BERLIN
ENCOUNTER

Books by T. Davis Bunn

The Quilt
The Gift

The Maestro
The Presence
Promises to Keep
Riders of the Pale Horse

The Priceless Collection
Secret Treasures of Eastern Europe

1. *Florian's Gate*
2. *The Amber Room*
3. *Winter Palace*

Rendezvous With Destiny

1. *Rhineland Inheritance*
2. *Gibraltar Passage*
3. *Sahara Crosswind*
4. *Berlin Encounter*

T. DAVIS BUNN

BERLIN ENCOUNTER

BETHANY HOUSE PUBLISHERS
MINNEAPOLIS, MINNESOTA 55438

This story is entirely a creation of the author's imagination. No parallel between any persons, living or dead, is intended.

Cover illustration by Joe Nordstrom

Published by Bethany House Publishers
A Ministry of Bethany Fellowship, Inc.
11300 Hampshire Avenue South
Minneapolis, Minnesota 55438

Printed in the United States of America.

Library of Congress Cataloging-in-Publication Data

Bunn, T. Davis, 1952–
    Berlin encounter / T. Davis Bunn.
        p.   cm. — (Rendezvous with destiny ; bk. 4)

    1. Berlin (Germany)—History—1945–1990—Fiction.
I. Title. II. Series: Bunn, T. Davis, 1952–   Rendezvous
with destiny ; 4.
PS3552.U4718B47   1995
813'.54—dc20   94–49222
ISBN 1–55661–382–2   CIP

This book is dedicated to

Patricia Bunn

and

E. Lee Bunn

with love

And to

Jeff and Lisa Jarema

With love and heartfelt
best wishes for a
joyful life together

T. DAVIS BUNN, originally of North Carolina, spent many years in Europe as an international business executive. Fluent in several languages, his successful career took him to over 40 countries of the world. But in recent years his faith and his love of writing have come together for a new direction in his life, and *Berlin Encounter* is his thirteenth published novel. This extraordinarily gifted novelist is able to craft high-powered political and historical fiction, as well as simple yet compelling stories like *The Quilt* and *The Gift*. Davis' aim is to entertain and inspire. He and his wife, Isabella, currently make their home in Henley-On-Thames, England.

Chapter One

The lead plane rocked its wings once, twice, but no voice cut through the radio static. There was too much risk of being overheard to speak unless there was an emergency. And if there was an emergency, they were all goners anyway.

The big Halifax bomber then lifted its wings toward the moonless night sky, and the pilot of Jake Burnes's glider jammed back the release catch. There was a loud *thunk* as the cable jolted from its hook, and a shudder ran through the glider as they caught the tow plane's parting downdraft. Then the bomber disappeared into the night sky, and the loudest noises were the glider's creaking frame and the wind.

Their glider was an enormous British Horsa, designed to transport either a full squad of heavily armed troops or a small tank. Jake glanced behind him, saw that the two trucks and their unmarked bundles were riding steady. Behind the load, all was empty shadows and rushing wind. He turned back to the glider's narrow windows, squinted out, saw nothing but gathering rain droplets. They were flying through clouds.

The glider jerked violently. Jake gripped his seat with white-knuckle panic. The plane seesawed, the wooden frame groaning with protest. But nothing gave.

Jake glanced at the pilot seated next to him. The man remained utterly unconcerned. But Jake took little comfort in the pilot's calm. He had already learned that glider pilots had their nerves surgically removed during training.

"Ten minutes," the man said, his voice a casual high-class British drawl. "Best strap in."

They escaped from the clouds, but the droplets only grew larger. This was what the powers that be had wanted, a rainy night with low-lying clouds. That way, though the tow plane's mighty engines would be heard, spotting would be impossible. Their exact landing point was relatively unimportant because no one would be there to meet them. All they needed was a flat and isolated field.

Jake squinted through the rain-blurred windscreen, tried hard not to let his fear take over. How the pilot was supposed to find a landing field in these conditions had never been fully explained.

The Horsa transport glider had been used in various World War II battles, including the D-Day invasion. That had been Jake's first thought when he heard how his mission was to begin, and the knowledge had stifled his protests a little. His younger brother, his last living relative, had died in the assault on Omaha Beach, and even that minimal connection left Jake feeling a little closer to the family he still sorely missed. The glider was canvas-covered wood with only the most rudimentary of controls, built as cheaply as possible. Which made perfect sense. Transport gliders were seldom used more than once.

Jake grimaced as another rain-swept gust buffeted

their glider. He wished he had protested after all.

"Here we are," the pilot shouted over the wind. "Just the ticket."

Jake leaned forward and searched as hard as he could, saw only faint patches of shadows. "Shouldn't we check closer down and make sure?"

"Nonsense," the pilot retorted loudly, and nosed the giant glider downward. "That field is level as a cricket pitch. Couldn't ask for a more delightful spot."

Jake saw that further argument was useless. He gripped an overhead guide wire with one hand and his seat with the other, braced his feet, and sent a frantic prayer lofting upward.

An endless moment of rushing wind and drumming rain and jerking, jouncing downward flight, then shadows coalesced into tight squares that looked far too small to ever catch and safely hold a plane like theirs. Down farther, leveling and pulling back and nosing up and slowing more, and Jake had a sudden notion that he might actually live through this after all.

Then a tree appeared out of nowhere, reached out great shadow-limbs, and neatly tore off one wing.

The glider hit the ground almost level, then the remaining wing dug into the earth and wrenched off with the sound of screaming timber and ripping canvas. The plane went into a gentle sideways skid, held upright by the weight of its cargo. The Horsa dug a deep furrow in the boggy soil, as forward progress was gradually braked by whipping through a field of ripening wheat.

Then they stopped.

Jake looked over at the pilot, took his first full-sized breath since the nose had pointed downward, and laughed.

The pilot, a jaunty ace with sunburned cheeks and a sidewise grin, replied, "I think that went rather well."

Jake unclenched his death's grip. "At least we're alive."

"Precisely." The pilot snapped his belt, stood, stretched his back, said, "I suppose we'd best be moving along, then."

"Right behind you."

Even though it was early June, the rain that sluiced through the two great gaping holes in the fuselage was bitterly cold. Jake kept his flight jacket zipped up tight to his collar as he set his shoulder alongside the pilot's and strained to open the loading door. But their landing had knocked the portal off its hinges and jammed it tight. Jake heaved with all his might and strained until he felt he was about to blow a gasket, but the door did not budge.

Finally the pilot leaned back and took a gasping breath. "Rather a bother, that."

"What about—" Jake stopped, tensed, and listened. For a moment, all he heard was the sound of rain drumming on taut canvas. Then there it was again. Voices shouting from a distance.

The pilot hissed, "Is that German?"

"Can't tell." He strained, listened further, said, "Maybe. Maybe not. Could be Russian."

"Then it is time, as they say, to scarper." The pilot leaped for the rear truck. "Only one shot here," he said. "If your motor doesn't catch, you come in with me. I'll do likewise."

Jake nodded, climbing aboard the front truck. Just what he liked in a jam, to find his back watched by a man who knew how to think on his feet. He found the starter button, pumped the gas pedal, turned, and when the pilot gave him a thumbs up, he fired the engine.

The motor whirred, grumbled, and roared to life.

Even above the pair of racing engines, Jake could hear voices rising to shouts of alarm. He gave no time to thought, however. No time. He raced his engine once more, unsure what the pilot had in mind, but at this point ready for anything.

The pilot revved his motor to full bore, then jammed his truck into reverse and rammed it straight through the back of the plane.

Without a moment for caution, Jake followed suit.

There was a rending, scraping shriek, then a moment of sailing through air, then a squishy thud. Tires spun, engine roared, wheels found purchase and propelled the vehicle in a tight circle. In reverse. At a pace far too fast for driving through a field of wheat at two o'clock in the morning.

Jake braked, shouted at the gears when he could not find first, looked up in time to see the second great truck come barreling out of the night headed straight for his door. The pilot managed to spin his vehicle out of range at the very last moment, sent a cheery "Beg your pardon" across the distance, and disappeared into the field.

Jake revved his engine and followed suit.

Only to find himself plowing straight through a squad of soldiers.

He would have been hard put to say who was more startled, he at the sight of these armed men appearing out of nowhere, or they at the vision of a roaring truck parting the wheat and barreling down on them without lights. Rifles were tossed to the heavens as soldiers dived in every conceivable direction. Jake jammed the pedal to the floor and kept right on going.

The field gave way to a rutted road which he found and lost and found again, in the meantime dismantling the corner of what, given the squawks of protest his passage caused, he could only assume was a chicken coop. He did not stop to investigate.

It was only when he was a good hour down the road that Jake finally decided it was time to put on his lights, slow down, and try to find out exactly where he was.

Chapter Two

S it down, Colonel." The hard-eyed gentleman with whom Jake met two weeks before his departure had worn civilian clothes with the ease of a courtier. "I understand you speak German."

Jake took the offered chair, knew immediately that he was dealing with one of the new types. Quentin Helmsley was a man who had not served in the war, who knew how to fire a gun because he had studied a book and practiced at a firing range. "Some."

"Records I have here say it's more than that."

"What records would those be?"

The man simply patted the closed folder under his hands. "Three and a half years of German at college before signing up, just one semester shy of a degree, isn't that right? Then your operations at the Badenburg garrison after the war's end showed near fluency. Quite impressive, I must say, your initiative to stop the cholera epidemic. Understand you're finally to receive a medal for that one. Rightly so."

If Jake's months of training had taught him any-thing, it was that these nonmilitary types treated in-formation like jewels, to be treasured and displayed only at the right moment. "Showed fluency according to whom?"

The man ignored his question. "I take it you have been following the news lately, Colonel?"

"Some." Force fed, more like. Jake's recent training had been haphazard in many respects, but not in this one. Daily seminars, each led by masters in the field of international assessment, focused on teaching a select few to see the globe as a continually evolving entity. Political trends and economic interactions and military power flowed like the wind, sometimes quiet and stable, other times raging with hurricane force. Jake was being taught to read these earthly elements like a weatherman watched the sky, predicting where the next tempest would erupt, being there to observe and prepare. The greatest threat now facing them was of Soviet domination in Eastern Europe. The wartime alliance with Russia had collapsed into mutual suspicion, and the world's balance of power was shifting dramatically.

"You are one of the highest ranking officers we are bringing in at this point," the gentleman said, switching gears. It was another action Jake had observed, this desire to keep their quarry off balance at all times. It did not matter that he and Jake were on the same side. The nature of the business required reactions that were so ingrained as to be automatic. This was one of the things that bothered Jake most about his training. He liked his reflexes just the way they were.

"There is some debate as to whether our man in Paris made an error in offering you an administrative post. You see, we prefer to bring our top men up from within."

Administrative. Jake kept his face impassive, but

grimaced internally. You chain me to a desk, bub, and I'm out of here.

"You were scheduled to return to Washington for six months of local, shall we say, orientation. We have been wondering if you might be willing to put this off for a bit of field duty." The man straightened, as though preparing for an argument. "Strictly off the record, Colonel, a successful stint in the field would improve your position considerably with the boys back home."

Jake hid his growing interest. "So what do they call the action I saw before you offered me this job?"

"*Independent* field action." His face showed a flicker of distaste. "Quite successful, such as it was. This has swayed many in your favor. But not all."

Including you, Jake thought, his feelings hardening to genuine dislike.

"A stint as a field operative under standard supervision would mean a great deal to the fence-sitters, I assure you."

"Sounds reasonable," Jake said, trying to put a reluctant note to his voice. In truth, the thought of spending six months playing trained seal for the bigwigs back in Washington held about as much appeal as brushing his teeth with battery acid.

They were seated in a grand country estate in the county of Surrey, some thirty miles outside London. Through the tall window behind the man's desk, Jake had a fine view of rolling countryside, the green broken only by a single church steeple poking through distant trees. During most of the war, the country estate had served as a U.S. command post. After D-Day it had been left more or less empty. Now it saw duty as a training-and-admin center for Allied operatives engaged in the infant science of intelligence gathering.

The manor house itself was huge, with two wings containing fifty bedrooms each, and a central portion longer than a football field. The Americans had been assigned two floors in the west wing and used hardly half the space.

Jake found it comforting to observe that work here seemed to proceed in the same haphazard way as it had in the army, making progress almost despite itself. NATO was now up and running, at least on paper, and as part of this show of unity, operatives were now being trained jointly. At least, that was what was supposed to be happening. In truth, Jake saw little of his counterparts from other nations except in class, and clearly some of them had been given strict orders to keep all other nationals at arm's length. They treated a simple hello as a threat to national security.

Jake did not mind keeping his distance. Although the majority of his fellow trainees were only a few years younger than he, most had missed the war. He found almost all of them, including the Americans, naive and overly serious. Their eager earnestness left him feeling like some crusty, battle-weary soldier. He had stopped wearing his uniform. The display of medals tended to halt traffic in the halls.

His teachers came from every country in western Europe; this was the primary reason that Jake relished his time here. They were older and had seen duty of one sort or another, many transferring from frontline service to intelligence and back again several times. They treated Jake as an equal and opened their vast stores of wisdom to him without reserve.

Idly Jake fingered the invitation in his pocket and allowed his mind to wander away from this frosty fellow and his maneuverings. The invitation had arrived that morning, engraved and embossed with a floral design, requesting the honor of his presence and that of his wife Sally at the Marseille wedding of Major Pierre Servais and Mademoiselle Jasmyn Coltrane. Jake already knew of the upcoming nuptials, of course, since he was to be best man. Sally had pasted stars around the date on their calendar at home, a not-too-subtle reminder that under no circumstances was Jake to let his new responsibilities come between him and his friends.

One excellent aspect of this new duty was being able to see his wife at work as well as at home. He and Sally had been married just over a year now, but a glimpse of her in the grand hallways still caused something to catch in his throat.

After heartrending months of separation, a breathless reunion, and a romantic engagement in Paris, they had returned to Karlsruhe—where Jake was commander of the U.S. garrison—for the wedding. From there they had expected a quick move to England for Jake's new intelligence position. But the transfer had not been as swift as planned, for the army had proved most reluctant to release him from his command. Jake had only caught faint wisps of the smoke, but it appeared that the battle had raged all the way back to the Pentagon before a final broadside from War Department level had cleared him for action.

Sally had found an excellent posting right there within NATO Intelligence headquarters, working for the top British administrator. A husband and wife working within the same operation was certainly not standard operating procedure, but Sally's top-secret clearance and her experience with general staff made her a prize beyond measure. They had rented a small country cottage five miles from the base and filled every nook and gable with the joy of their newfound love.

Jake's attention returned to the man behind the desk when he realized he was being asked a question. Quentin Helmsley had recently arrived from Washington. The senior staff either treated him with great respect or quiet disdain, depending on what they thought of the power he represented. He was asking, "By any chance, Colonel, have you traveled the region of Mecklenburg-Vorpommern?"

"Never set foot in it, so far as I know."

"A pity," Helmsley said. "We have had, ah, several setbacks in this area recently."

Jake searched his memory, located the German state as lying just east of Hamburg, the northernmost state in the Russian sector. "You mean you've lost your local men."

The fellow did not deny it. "Stalin's edicts have proven to be just as harsh in practice as they sound in rhetoric. This is causing no end of distress throughout the regions now under his control, especially Eastern Europe. Entire towns are being awakened in the middle of the night, herded into trucks, and driven off, never to be seen again."

Jake nodded. This he had already heard. Firsthand accounts of Stalin's mass resettlement operations were now filtering out to the West.

"These policies are now being applied in increasingly harsh measure to the Russian-controlled region of Germany," Helmsley went on, "and the Russians have been setting up puppet regimes. This process was formerly limited to the local level, which did not bother us very much. But it is now being extended to the establishment of regional and even a quasi-national administration. And all of the new officials, so far as we can tell, are German Communists who either fled Hitler's Germany and hid in Russia or spent the war years locked in concentration camps. The majority of these returning Communists see all the people under their control as having sold out to Hitler and thereby responsible for their own persecution. They *hate* their own countrymen, or many of them do, and use their new powers with truly brutal force."

This was news. Despite his recently acquired caution, Jake found himself growing interested.

Helmsley sensed this and gave a small smile of satisfaction. "It also appears that there is soon to be a re-settlement of German scientists whom Russia finds useful. And this is what concerns us. There is a town in Mecklenburg-Vorpommern called Rostock, about thirty kilometers north of the capital, Schwerin. It was there that Hitler's scientists developed the most sophisticated rockets in the world."

Rockets. Jake gave a single small nod. Of course. It would have to be something big to risk going in where other men had already been lost.

"Several German scientists escaped from Rostock just before the war," Helmsley went on. "Through our contacts, we were able to get several messages to those who remained. As a result, we have managed to entice two of the remaining experts to join us."

"You want me to risk my neck," Jake said, "to rescue a couple of Nazi scientists?"

"One of them is a Nazi," Helmsley admitted with a wintry smile. "Former Nazi, in any case. And needing their minds does not mean that we must necessarily like them, Colonel."

The idea of going in to rescue an enemy, even a former enemy, unsettled him mightily. And this was a surprise. His work at Karlsruhe and before that at Badenburg had brought him in contact with more than one former Nazi, and he thought he had put the old feelings behind him. But now, abruptly, Jake found his Christian principles and his awareness of new political realities doing battle with a vision of his brother lying dead on the Normandy beaches. "And they really have information we don't have?"

"I assure you," Helmsley replied. "We would not go to all this trouble unless it were absolutely necessary. From what we have gathered, this group has managed to forge a full generation ahead of us in rocket research. All of London bears witness to the effectiveness of their flying bombs." Helmsley inspected him a long moment, then demanded, "We need these two men, Colonel. Will you go in?"

"Go in?" Despite the inner turmoil, he did not have to think it over. "Sure."

There was an instant of hesitation, as though Helmsley was finally forced to see Jake as something other than just a potential operative to be swayed to his purpose. "I was informed that your abilities were matched by a capacity to think on your feet."

Jake had difficulty keeping the surge of excitement from showing. No need to let the guy know he'd have paid a year's wages to work in the field again. "What can you tell me about the place where they're kept?"

"Operations will brief you on details. It appears, however, that we were never able to do this particular facility much damage with our bombing campaigns. Part of your objective will be to, shall we say, rattle the Russians' scientific cage a little." Helmsley tapped a nervous finger on the closed file, then went on, "I must tell you that having several of our men disappear has troubled us. We cannot be sure, but it appears that they were not apprehended as spies, simply picked up with the local population and carted off to goodness knows where. But we cannot wait for them to return, Colonel. We must bring the two key scientists out now. Time has become of the essence."

"You think the Russians might move them back into their own territory," Jake surmised.

"What your other supporters have said of you appears to be correct," he said, the look of respect deepening. "There is one other thing. I don't suppose you would mind carrying in a load of contraband, would you?"

"I guess not. What did you have in mind?"

The glimmer was replaced by cynical humor as he replied, "Bibles."

Chapter Three

J ake was driving slowly enough to spot the disused forest track and pull off in one smooth motion. He saw no other headlights on the lonely predawn road, and he had not passed a house in ten minutes. Still, he pulled the truck into a tight nest formed by a dozen fir trees, then snaked back through the woods on foot. When he reached the road he squatted in the cold darkness, rain dropping from the hood of his poncho, and searched the shadows. He waited and watched, no reason to hurry except his own discomfort. The war had taught him that errors made in haste sometimes left no escape except death.

To keep him company as he waited in the wet woods, straining to ensure that none of the trees or bushes grew legs and approached, he thought of Sally. She had refused to see him off at the airfield, and he had not objected. He had no desire whatsoever to share their leave-taking with anyone, much less a bunch of gawking military types.

Jake's battle-trained reflexes had returned after almost two years of disuse, permitting him to reset his internal clock in anticipation of night action and to sleep the afternoon away. He had awakened toward dusk to find her stretched out on the pillow next to his, watching him with that calm, strong gaze which was hers and hers alone.

"I hate to see you go," were the first words he heard upon awakening. "Just thinking about it leaves me feeling like a part of me has gone missing. But I've come to see something as I've been lying here. Something really important."

Jake rolled over and faced her fully. He resisted the urge to touch her, knowing she did not want it. Not just then. "Tell me."

"Maybe I knew it already. Maybe I saw it when I was back in the States shepherding those generals around and you were back here. But it wasn't clear to me then. I just knew my life wasn't complete without you. Now, all of a sudden, I understand."

She propped her head up with one hand and said in a voice that was soft and yielding, yet utterly practical. "It had to be you, Jake. All my life I've been waiting to meet the man who rides the wind, the man who travels the paths that no one else even wants to find. The man filled with faith and mystery and strength and action." Her voice quivered, but she forced herself to finish, "And danger."

"Sally—"

"Wait, let me finish. I knew you had the strength and that special focus that is all your own. This is what appealed to me from the very beginning. But I've been lying here, waiting for you to wake up and hold me and then get up and walk through that door, and now I understand that this really is part of it. Now and for the rest of our lives." She shifted, made uncomfortable by the raw truth. "Oh, I don't know if you'll stay with this work. I don't really care, to tell you the truth. But

I know that you'll always find something that requires more from you than most other people are willing to give.

Jake found himself unable to speak. He just lay and watched her and marveled at her ability to see to the very depths of him.

"This is who you are. Living life to the fullest for you means living beyond the borders, going into the places where others are afraid to walk, maybe even to see. Only now there are two of us, Jake." Her eyes welled up at this, and a single tear escaped to descend in gentle sorrow across her cheek. "You aren't alone anymore."

"I'll be careful," he whispered, and reached across to catch the tear. It rested on his finger, an incredible gift of her love.

"That's not enough, Jake. You were always careful. That's why you're still here. But now you need to re-member that you carry two hearts with you every-where you go." She reached for him then, pressing her entire length to him, melding to his form and holding him close. "Our two lives are woven together now, my beloved. Two destinies follow in each footstep you take. So you've got to take more than care. You must promise to return."

She drew back just a little, to meet his eyes again. "I will learn to let you go with love and confidence. But you must always return. Always."

That same evening, when Jake had returned to headquarters to complete his preparations, he had been approached by one of the senior administrators.

Harry Grisholm was another American, whose misshapen body disguised a rapier-keen mind. He had started as a field operative, but a bad night-landing in Holland had shattered hips and legs so badly that neither could be completely corrected. But instead of returning to a desk job and well-earned honors, Harry had seen out the rest of the war coordinating clandestine radio operations throughout northern Holland.

He walked with a rolling lurch, his oversized head bobbing like a poorly strung marionette. Months of agony had etched deep lines across his forehead and out from his eyes and mouth. Yet his cheerful demeanor had altered the creases into permanent smile lines. "What did you think of our Mister Helmsley?"

"Made me wonder if maybe I hadn't made a mistake taking this job," Jake replied.

"He and his kind are the wave of the future, Jake. Best you get used to them."

"This is supposed to cheer me up?"

"Listen, my friend. In our business, we must be the ultimate realists. Our very existence depends upon it." He fastened Jake with a piercing ice-blue gaze. "He has been shaped by his background just as you have been shaped by yours. Both have pluses and minuses, my level-headed friend. He would never make a field operative and would most certainly never handle men very well. His is the kind who would vastly prefer to fire every human being in the service and strive for ever more sophisticated electronic devices."

"So?"

"So a service such as our own will never survive and do its job when given over to people like this," Harry said patiently. "Field operatives are the service's infantry, often maligned but always needed. It is only through the eyes and ears of trusted men there on the spot that we shall ever truly understand what our electronic devices have gathered."

He reached up and thumped Jake's chest. "At the same time, my friend, you would never be happy doing our man Helmsley's job. Never. Not in a million years would you spend your days running from office to office, passing on just the right information to just the right ear, making sure that your budget remains intact, sitting through day after day of committee meetings, trying to advise presidents and their aides about international crises which have not yet happened and thus are not urgent in their eyes—"

"A nightmare," Jake declared. "I'd rather walk across a field of live coals in my bare feet."

"Precisely. What our man Helmsley fails to realize, just as it has escaped you up to now, is that you need each other. You *complement* each other." Harry stopped and waited, making sure his words were sinking in. "The world is made up of a myriad of peoples. You will do far better looking for those who share your objectives than trying to live only with those who see the world through your perspective. And once you learn that lesson, you will need to teach it to the equally stubborn Helmsley."

"That makes sense," Jake agreed.

"You're most welcome." Harry gave him a frosty smile which did not descend from his eyes. "Would you accept a further bit of advice?"

"From you? Always."

"Your orders and your instructions have been made extra complex, I am sorry to say, because a few of these fellows here feel threatened by your record, and would just as soon see you fail."

"I thought maybe something like that was going on." Jake snapped the catches on the leather satchel he had been packing. "Still, they all seemed to make good sense."

"They make good sense to you *here*." Harry's eyes were keen with the strength of hard-earned wisdom. "Take it from me, Jake. A successful field operative is one who has the sense to divert from orders when the situation merits it." He patted Jake's arm. "And a good field operative, my friend, is one who survives."

Twenty minutes of searching shadows to either side of the rain-drenched road satisfied Jake that the coast was as clear as it would ever get. Twice he had watched army convoys trundle by, but neither had appeared to be on alert. The woods had remained still and wet and empty. Jake returned to his truck just as dawn began to push away the grudgingly stubborn night. He felt chilled to the bone.

While water heated on a paraffin stove, Jake began the job of changing his own and the truck's identity.

First he stripped off the truck's green army-issue top, which proved not to be made of canvas at all, but rather of flimsy parachute silk. He then peeled off the green sidings, which were not wood and metal, but burlap stiffened with multiple layers of paint and nailed into place. The U.S. Army stars disappeared from the truck doors, as did the army license plates and stenciling across front and back. Finally the camouflaging was peeled off the hood and cabin top and the rear loading platform.

Despite the low-lying clouds, the argument had

gone, there was still a chance that their landing would be observed. So both trucks were to depart from the landing site declaring to all the world that they were indeed standard army issue.

Jake pulled the shovel from the back of the truck, walked to a clearing beyond the trees, and began to dig. By the time the hole was deep enough, he was sweating and breathing hard. He returned to the truck, stripped off the sergeant's uniform in which he had traveled, and dressed from the clothes in his satchel. He then buried both the uniform and the truck's false covers. He strew pine needles and sticks over the fresh earth, then stepped back and surveyed the scene. It would not stand a close inspection, but it would probably do.

He returned to the truck and his breakfast, standard fare for that region—chicory coffee, hard cheese, day-old bread, a couple of wizened apples. As he ate, Jake inspected himself in the truck's cracked side mirror. What he saw made him grin with satisfaction.

The clothes matched the truck's new identity, that of a small-time trader. Jake's cheap black-leather jacket crinkled and squeaked with each movement. His black turtleneck and dark shapeless trousers were matched by his three-day growth and a haircut which had raised shrieks of dismay from Sally the day he had brought it home. He looked shrewd, hard, tired, and thoroughly dishonest.

The truck looked in wretched shape, at least unless someone did a careful inspection under the hood. The sides were scarred and weather-beaten, the canvas top so patched that it was hard to tell what the original color had been, the front end battered to a paintless pulp. It looked like a thousand other trucks trundling through Germany's war-ravaged landscape, dregs discarded by retreating armies, scarred by thousands of hard-fought miles.

But the muddy tires were the best that money could buy, the tank three times normal size, the suspension perfect. The gears meshed like a Swiss watch, and the well-muffled motor was tuned and tightened until it could easily push the truck to over a hundred miles an hour, even in four-wheel drive.

Not to mention the fact that spaced over the truck's frame were two secret compartments designed to escape even the most careful of inspections.

As Jake repacked his meager utensils, he gave a passing thought to the British pilot. The man had been ordered to round up four of their remaining operatives, people considered to be in the worst danger of being resettled and lost forever. He had more than nine hundred kilometers to cover behind Soviet lines, with the Russian army patrols constantly on the move. Jake did not envy him the challenge.

As he started the engine and pulled out the compass concealed beneath the dash, Jake had a fleeting image of the pilot thinking the same thing about Jake's assignment.

Chapter Four

The journey to Rostock went so well that Jake found himself mildly disappointed.

Their landing zone had turned out to be a thin strip of farmland separating the dangerously sandy Baltic shoreline from the hilly forests and industrial towns of inner Mecklenburg-Vorpommern. Jake trundled down an empty brick-and-mud country lane with a carefully battered road map in his lap. The rain had lessened with the dawn, and the wind had freshened to gusty squalls.

He drove slowly, looking for what should be the turnoff to Rostock. Jake squinted down at the map, felt the dismay of a lost traveler. He had a fleeting image of perhaps wandering along some uncharted road, the glider having been set free a thousand miles off course and depositing them in a land so far from where he was supposed to be that the map was utterly useless.

Then in the distance he spotted a great metal crane, the sort used for unloading ships, and suddenly the map came into focus. The road was identified, his target pinpointed. A few miles later he crossed a rise, and the port of Rostock spread out beneath him.

The harbor was a mere shadow of its former self.

Four of the five giant loading cranes had been reduced
to hulks of steel and slag. Of the dozen port buildings,
none had their roofs intact, three had been totally destroyed, and another four were so pitted and scarred
that he could watch men moving the pallets about inside. Roads and rails surrounding the port were stud-
ded with shell holes. The ships waiting patiently at
dockside appeared to be in equally bad shape. Jake
spent a long moment inspecting the scene, then
gunned his motor and drove on.

His way took him down and around the city's western side, skirting the main roads and most activity.
Still, what he saw depressed him. Little repair work
appeared to be going on. Two and a half years after the
war's end, and most of the damaged homes and factories still bore only the most basic reconstructions.
The contrast with the frenetic activity surrounding
every town and city in the western sectors was stag-
gering.

Most bomb-splintered windows had been replaced
with plywood or cardboard; Jake saw almost no glass.
Crumbling walls had been propped up with uncured
tree trunks still bearing leaves and limbs. Roads were
pocked with shell holes filled with dirt and gravel or
simply left in their dismal state. Wires and cables remained strewn everywhere, which more than likely
meant that electricity had not been generally restored.
Jake found this remarkable. The entire region around
Karlsruhe, where he had served, had returned to full
power within a year of the peace settlement. How else
were the factories to run, giving people jobs and the
economy a chance to get back on its feet?

It was hard to tell much from the people. They
looked grim, but so did most Germans. Five hard years

of war, followed by total defeat, had left scars which would not fade so swiftly. But he had the impression that there was more hunger here than in the western sectors, more hardship, more despair.

And less traffic. Jake's was one of the few vehicles he saw upon the road which did not bear military markings. He saw only an occasional car, and the few civilian trucks he spotted looked as bad as his. So did the scattering of trams and buses, all stuffed to the point that passengers hung from the stairs and outer railings and children crammed onto the back runners.

The closer he drew to the town, the more stares he drew. Some looked with hostility, others with outright envy. Here was a truck. Privately owned. A man wealthy enough to have both transport and fuel and some reason for both.

He arrived at the unmarked crossing with vast relief at having escaped those hostile eyes and at not having passed a checkpoint yet. The longer he could remain unchecked, Jake reasoned, the less chance there would be of his being connected to the mysterious arrival of a British glider bearing two trucks with U.S. Army markings.

Jake stowed the map back under his seat. It was of no use to him now. This road and all that was yet to come had been committed to memory before he had left England.

Jake drove two miles farther and reached the last farm before entering the woods. He checked his watch and pulled off. His instructions were to arrive at the installation's outer gates precisely at noon. If not that day, then the next, or the day after. But only at noon.

Jake did not need to see the people to know that eyes were watching him. He climbed down, stretched his back, proceeded to make and eat an early lunch. Calm, casual, easygoing, but watchful. A trader operating on his own had every reason these days to seek a solitary lay-by before stopping.

Twenty minutes later the farmer finally stepped from behind his ramshackle barn. He stood for a long moment before walking slowly over, using a sharpened pitchfork as a staff. Jake turned and watched him approach, but did not stop eating. He returned the farmer's suspicious greeting, decided he might as well give his story one trial run before hitting the big time.

"You a trader?" The farmer tried for nonchalance, but his squinty gaze continually flitted toward the back flap.

"Feed and seeds," Jake replied, his tone laconic. "Some tools. Pots and pans. Boots."

"Boots," the man said, and glanced down at his own feet. His shoes were bound to his ankles with twine. Newspaper poked from holes at the toe. The squinty gaze rose and leveled on Jake. "Where you from?"

"Everywhere," Jake said, knowing his accent was rough, but hoping the instructors had been correct when they said he did not sound like an American. Americans tended to mangle the tones of other languages, they had told him. Jake had a careful ear, holding the tones as correct as he could. He sounded foreign, but not from any particular place. Dutch, perhaps. Or Hungarian who had learned Swiss German. Or Danish, except his coloring was too dark. "I've spent my whole life traveling, buying and selling."

Envy flashed across the farmer's seamed features. "Been here all my life. Watched the world come and go, I have. Trouble and woe, only things that have remained."

Jake grunted, figuring that a man who made his living off small-time deals would not have much time for the troubles of others. He reached into the back, carefully shielding the payload from the farmer's prying eyes, and drew forward one of the two sacks bearing boots. Both the canvas sacks and the boots themselves had been brought to England from the western sector of Germany, as had all the other manmade products.

Jake unleashed the neck catch of one bag and drew out samples of recovering Germany's workmanship. Each segment of the boots had been cut from different-colored leather, the stitching was irregular, the eyelets were uneven, and the soles were made of tire rubber. But from the farmer's expression Jake realized they were far better than anything he had been offered recently.

"We don't have money for boots," a woman's voice announced sharply.

The farmer did not look around as he accepted one of the boots, handed Jake the pitchfork, and raised one foot to compare the sizes. "The trader's got pans."

The woman took an involuntary step forward. "Took all our pots, they did. All of them."

"Been cooking on a coal griddle and a shovel blade," the farmer said, giving the second shoe a careful inspection. "*Ach du lieber,* I grow mighty tired of fry-grease."

Jake's only reaction was to reach back inside and heave close the nearest crate. He lifted the first handle, unwrapped the burlap used to keep the pots from rattling, hefted the great cooking-pot and said as he had been instructed, "These come dear."

The woman was unable to conceal her desire. The farmer inspected his wife and sighed in defeat, "How much for the boots and the pan?"

"We don't have money," the woman warned. "It's gone."

"We sell to the commissar," the farmer said, his eyes pleading, though simple pride kept it from his voice. "Have to. They pay in scrip. Lets us buy supplies, if there are any, which isn't often."

"All the farm is listed," the woman said bitterly, grasping the handle from Jake and clasping the pot to her chest. "Everything we own, or what's left. Every cow, every chicken, every tool. Can't let you have an animal."

Jake bit back the urge to give them the goods, said simply, "What can you trade?"

Thirty minutes later he drove away, feeling for the first time that he just might make this whole thing work. His tank was topped off with twenty liters of fuel siphoned from the farmer's worn-out tractor. The truck was sweetly perfumed by a quarter ring of home-made cheese and half a loaf of fresh-baked bread. Two jars of honey nestled within straw in his glove box, and on the seat beside him rode two dozen newly laid eggs.

Which was why, when he approached the sentry guarding the derelict control station and did not see his contact, he leaned from his window and said as casually as he could muster, "Got any need for fresh food?"

Before the soldier's evident hunger could descend from his eyes to his tongue, a second man stepped from the sentry house. This one was dressed in the blue uniform of the political officer. "What's this, what's this?"

Jake watched the soldier stiffen to attention, saw

the disappointment which could not be masked. He made mental note of this as he slid from the cab. If soldiers at key installations were going hungry, things must indeed be bad. "Farmer up the road said I might find a buyer for some fresh goods."

"All produce is to be sold directly to the commissary and given out according to passbook regulations," the officer snapped. He squinted at Jake. "What was the farmer's name?"

"Didn't say I bought anything from him. Just got directions, is all." He cocked a thumb at the open door. "You want the stuff or not?"

The political officer jerked his head around the door, and his eyes widened. "Eggs!"

"Two dozen, fresh as they come," Jake said, enjoying himself despite the risk. Maybe he had a knack for the world of high finance, if this present line of work gave out. "You take them all, I'll make you a good deal."

The officer raised himself up to full height, a shrewd glint appearing in his eyes. "These are legally licensed eggs?"

"They're mine," Jake replied, an edge creeping to his voice. "And they can be yours if you've got anything to offer besides—"

"You made it, good, good!" His contact scuttled through the sentry point. "Herr Thalle, this is the trader I mentioned, the one with the tools!"

The political officer saw his hopes fading. Greed turned to sullen anger. "Not to mention unlicensed eggs."

The scientist wore a white lab coat turned gray with age and hand washing. He gave a false little laugh. "Ah, but what are a few eggs among comrades?"

"I could have him thrown in jail for such a crime."

"Yes, but then where would we be? You know we've been waiting almost six months for these tools." Sweat beaded his upper lip as he turned to Jake and demanded, "You have them?"

"I might," Jake drawled, his eyes still on the political officer. The man was an officious little puppet, all spit and polish in his bright blue uniform with the silver buttons and the ribbons on his lapel. "Then again, I might have stashed them up the road a ways. Until I could see what kind of reception I was going to have here."

"An excellent reception!" The dark-haired scientist positively burst with nervous bonhomie. "We have been looking out for you now for over a month, haven't we, Herr Thalle?"

"Even so," the officer grumbled, "I still say we have no cause to deal with common criminals."

"Then I'll be on my way," Jake said, and turned back toward the truck.

"No, no, please, wait!" Frantically the scientist grabbed at his sleeve, his spectacles sliding down his nose in the process. He let go of Jake long enough to readjust the glasses, then slid between Jake and the cab. The smile was still there, but slipping around the edges. "Perhaps a small gift, a token, to the good Herr Thalle would ease our way through this misunderstanding, yes?"

A little smirk painted itself on the officer's face as he replied, "Perhaps."

"A bribe, you mean." Jake felt his hackles rise at giving this petty troublemaker anything. Still, he was blocking Jake's way inside. Reluctantly Jake turned to the cab and brought out four eggs. And as he placed them in the man's hands he brought his face in close and said with quiet menace, "I think that should be more than enough, don't you?"

Something in Jake's gaze caused the man to take a single step back before replying, "Sentry!"

"Sir."

"Take his papers for inspection." The officer then wheeled about and retreated to the sentry building with as much firmness as he could muster.

Jake reached back inside the cab, took another four eggs, reached to the sentry, and said quietly, "My papers."

In his haste to take the eggs, the sentry almost dropped his rifle.

The scientist said, "The tools are very heavy. We will need to draw the truck up alongside the second entrance." When the sentry nodded without looking up from his prize, Jake shoved the scientist inside the cab, slid in beside him, slammed the door, and drove on.

"That was awful," the scientist said. "Why were you so rough on Herr Thalle?"

"No small-time trader is going to be an easy mark for a worm like that," Jake replied. He glanced over at the heavily perspiring scientist. "You are Doctor Rolf Grunner?"

"Yes. And you?"

"Jake Burnes. Colonel, NATO Intelligence."

"What has taken you so long, Colonel?"

"Had to set things up, then wait for the weather," Jake said succinctly. "Where to?"

"There, beside those green doors. We have been waiting almost a month. Hans, Dr. Hechter, he almost gave up hope. Things have been increasingly difficult in the laboratories. The rumors have been constant. Again yesterday we heard that they were taking us to a new facility. One somewhere in Kazakhstan, I think they said." The scientist pointed and said, "Stop here."

At first glance Jake understood why wartime bombing of the facility had been so ineffectual. The great metal doors did not open into buildings at all, but rather into cliffs that protruded from a steep-sided hill like buttresses from a great sand and rock vessel. The only exposed points were the outbuildings, several of which were blackened hulks. The concrete launching strip was also pocked with hastily repaired holes. Jake eased up to the set of crumbling concrete stairs, cut the motor, and let the scientist slide out.

"Bring help," Jake said laconically, scouting the area.

The scientist paused. "What?"

"The tools weigh a lot," Jake said. "Get help. Like maybe the other scientist."

"Oh. Yes. Of course."

"And the money," Jake reminded him. "And calm down."

The scientist gave him a dazed look from behind his spectacles, then disappeared inside. Jake walked around to the back, let down the tailgate, started heaving out the four bulkiest sacks from his cargo.

In moving the sacks, he noticed the well-hidden lever which opened the first of the hidden bays. It was recessed into the side of the hold and looked like nothing more than an extension of one of the canvas top guide-poles. Only if it was twisted in a certain way and then pushed out rather than back would it pop open. The door itself was hidden beneath layers of oil and grime and burlap. As Jake eased the first of the heavy sacks to the earth, he found himself thinking of what lay inside the bay, and of the conversation he had with Harry Grisholm after learning what he would be carrying.

"Bibles," Jake had repeated. The more he had thought of it, the less he had liked it. "Helmsley threw it out like he was offering the good little doggie a bone."

"It was a mistake," Harry affirmed. Harry was the only other professed Christian among the staff, another reason Jake enjoyed working with him so much. "But then again, he is not used to working with a believer. I'm sure it leaves him feeling uncomfortable. Suddenly he's faced with something that doesn't fit comfortably into his perspective."

Jake eased back and grinned. "How am I supposed to stay mad when you're agreeing with me like that?"

"The fact that you and I must learn to work with such people does not mean that I necessarily care for the man and his ways," Harry replied.

"I hated the way he used my faith," Jake went on, but without animosity. "Like it was just another point to stick in my file and bring out whenever it suited him."

"Listen to me, Jake." Harry sat up as far as his diminutive stature would allow. "You are being confronted with one of the basic problems of intelligence work. It attracts people whose dispositions make them enjoy manipulating both people and information. In some cases, I am not sure that they actually see so great a difference between the two. This is not new, Jake. I am sure that when Moses sent the young men to spy out the tribes inhabiting the Promised Land, there were some who saw it as the opportunity of a life-time—not to do God's work, but to possess this knowl-edge and parlay it into personal power and status."

Jake took a seat across from Harry's chair. His friend's stunted legs barely reached the floor. "How do you stand it, Harry?"

"First of all, because I happen to believe in what I am doing. There *are* enemies out there. There *is* a need to do our work, and to do it well." Harry had the re-markable capacity to smile more broadly with his eyes alone than most people could with their entire face. "I have the feeling that you think the same way, Jake."

Jake thought it over, nodded slowly. "Maybe so."

"Then should we allow the discomfort of working with such people keep us from the job? Should we leave *any* field to people who do not hold to our own ideals? If we feel ourselves called to this work, should we ever permit another to turn us away?"

An imperious voice behind him demanded in lofty German tones, "And just what excuse do you have for keeping us waiting so long?"

Jake stiffened, eased himself up slowly, found him-self facing a tall man perhaps ten years older than he. His neatly cropped hair was so blond as to be almost white, his eyes pure Aryan blue, his jaw strong, his nose lifted high enough that he might look down upon Jake, his left cheek bearing a well-healed scar. It was, Jake knew, the result of a saber duel, the required mark of courage within upper-class Prussian families. "Doctor Hans Hechter?"

"*Professor* Doctor Hechter," the imperious voice corrected.

"Colonel Jake Burnes, U.S. Army. Currently operating with NATO Intelligence."

The man's chin raised another notch, granting him the angle to stare down his nose at Jake. "You have not answered my question."

Jake's eyes narrowed. The guy was already getting under his skin. "Preparations took a while. Then we had to wait for the weather to cooperate."

"I do not find that a reasonable response," the man snapped. "Do you have any idea how greatly you have inconvenienced me? No, of course you do not. Well, Colonel, it has been positively horrid."

"You cannot imagine," Jake responded dryly, "how this news affects me."

The dark-haired scientist stepped forward and said nervously, "Come, Hans, this is getting us nowhere."

"Quite right." The frosty visage nodded once, satisfied with the dressing down. "You are American?"

"I just said that."

"You don't sound American," he said suspiciously.

"Good." Jake inspected the man, wondered if he would be able to keep hold of his temper during the days to come. "Where is your beard and haircut?"

The lofty irritation returned. "Really, Colonel. Your people could not truly have expected a man of my standing to resort to such pettiness."

"This affects all our security," Jake said, tempted to leave the man behind.

"I have a hat he can wear," Dr. Grunner said with

a nervous desire to ease the tension. "And his beard will grow swiftly."

Jake locked eyes and wills with the blond man and had a sudden impression of this man standing with a gun on the hills above the Normandy beaches, watching as Jake's brother struggled in futility to land and find safety. Not some fellow Nazi, not some soldier with similar features, *this man*. The rage which filled him was so great and came so swiftly it almost blinded him. But before the anger was transformed to action, the doors leading into the hillside creaked open once more.

"And what is this?" The voice was scarcely above the level of a whisper, yet it had the effect of shaking the arrogant Dr. Hechter as Jake could not. The ice-blue eyes faltered, the shoulders hunched slightly. Jake glanced up, and understood.

Like the official at the main gates, this man also wore the blue uniform of the People's Police, the puppet officials of the occupying Soviet forces. But this was no ineffectual marionette. Instead, he was lean to the point of perpetual emaciation. Years of suffering had pressed his lips to thin bloodless lines, stripped his features of all softness, and turned his eyes to slits of gray-marble. "Well? I am waiting for an answer."

Jake shifted his gaze back to the blond scientist and stated flatly, "I don't care who you parade out here. I am not dropping my price one pfennig."

There was a slight relaxing of the officer's tight features. "A trader? Two of my top scientists are out wasting time with a trader?"

"He has our tools," Grunner said, picking up the thread.

Jake saw the officer's reaction, knew the way this

one would think. Life meant nothing to someone like him. Jake added swiftly, "Half of them. You want the others, you pay full for these. No talk, no threats. The price we agreed on."

"*I* agreed to nothing," the officer snapped. "And you, gypsy, you watch your tone or I'll call out the guard."

The blond scientist turned about and announced, "You know full well the condition of our machinery. It is vital that we receive these tools. *All* of them."

"I know that you are falling further and further behind schedule in your work," the officer snapped. "And when I see the way you waste your time, I can well understand why."

"You will address me as Herr Professor," the scientist responded icily. "Or you will not address me at all."

Dr. Grunner lifted a battered envelope from his coat pocket and brandished it between them. "We have the money," he cried. "Our tool budget has been approved for months. You yourself signed the requisition. But there have been no tools anywhere, for no price. And now he has come with exactly what we need."

The political officer radiated a viciously compacted disapproval. "Exactly? You are sure?"

"We would be," Dr. Hechter replied frostily, "if you would allow us to go about our business."

The disapproval focused into vengeful bile. "It may not be possible to shoot you as should happen to all Nazis, *Professor*. But punishment can be arranged if your attitude does not improve. You do not need both feet to perform your duties, for example. You would do well to remember that."

When the door had closed behind the officer, the

blond scientist said quietly, "Former Nazi."

Rolf Grunner took a shaky breath, said to Jake, "You truly have the tools?"

"The ones you requested in the last message we received before our man disappeared," Jake answered, his eyes still on the door. "That was too close."

"That man should be taken out and shot," Dr. Hechter said from beside him.

Jake found his own unreasoning anger resurfacing. "That would be your answer to everything, would it?"

The scientist jerked as though slapped, but before he could respond his colleague was between them. "Gentlemen, please, I beg you, our very lives hang in the balance here."

Jake took a breath, nodded. "Let's unload."

When the bulky sacks were piled at the landing on top of the stairs, Grunner handed over the money. "This was the amount the last communique told us to have. Exactly."

"I need to count it in case someone's watching." Jake bent over the packet, lowered his voice, said, "There are two grenades in each of the sacks, one smoke and one frag. If you have to use them indoors, be sure to crouch and cover your ears."

"I've never used a grenade before," Grunner stammered.

"Let's hope you don't have to learn tonight. If you do, it helps to pull the pin before you throw." Jake scanned the empty field across from the laboratory. "How is security?"

"Poor," Grunner replied, certain for once. "The guards are as badly paid and poorly treated as we are."

"That makes our job easier. I will be by this door at two minutes to midnight. Get here early enough to check and see if it's locked. If so, I will blow it just before the diversion is set to go. Wait ten paces back, or around a corner, in a doorway, anything that will give you protection." Jake stuffed the bills into his jacket. "There is a path about a kilometer and a half before the main gate. I saw it on the way in. It looks like an old road, and runs straight as an arrow through the forest in this direction."

"I know it," Dr. Grunner said. "It comes out on the other side of the launch-pad. They used it when they were constructing these halls."

Jake made a pretense of opening one of the sacks, pulling out a gleaming tool, holding it as though for inspection. "If anything happens and you have to get out early, anything, head for where that path intersects the main road toward town." Jake thrust a tool back inside. He tied the neck of the sack, nerves over what was coming making his motions jerky. "There will be a diversion set for precisely five minutes after midnight. Whatever happens, if for any reason we don't rendezvous, don't be here when it goes off."

Grunner nodded nervously. "What sort of diversion?"

Jake turned back toward the truck. "Something loud."

"Just one minute, Colonel," Hechter said, stopping his progress toward the truck. The blond scientist stared at him, his lofty superiority back in force. "You really don't expect me to carry my own cases all the way through the forest."

"Your cases?" Jake shook his head in disbelief. "I don't expect you to carry them at all." Before the man could respond, he swung behind the wheel, started the engine, said through the open window, "Midnight. Be ready."

Chapter Five

S ally had never seen Harry Grisholm so angry.

She had been working at her desk when he arrived, trying to ignore her aching sense of loss. Adjusting to Jake's absence had been much harder than she expected. Before he had left, when she had thought about the mission at all, she had seen it as a shorter version of her own trip to America with the generals. But the reality had turned out far different from her expectations. Perhaps it was because Jake was the one who had done the leaving this time, perhaps because of the danger inherent in his mission, perhaps because she was more accepting of her own love. Whatever the reason, his absence was pure agony.

Being home was too much for her to bear alone. The lack of him was with her everywhere. So she had taken to spending more and more time in the office, surrounding herself both with work and with people who knew more about his mission than she did.

Jake had told her what he was going to do. That had been one of his departing gifts. If the intelligence forces themselves had granted her top-secret classification, he had reasoned, why on earth shouldn't he use it for something this important? She had listened and struggled to hide her anxiety, knowing that it had to be done, knowing that he was going, knowing that to weigh him down with her own worries would only increase the risk.

Her office was connected to one of the three administrators assigned to coordinate NATO Intelligence activities. Commander Randolf formerly led a British antisubmarine squadron. His demeanor was as rigid and unbending as his sparse frame. The sea-green eyes which peered out from beneath his bushy brows had the singular intensity of two minutely adjusted gun barrels.

Yet even his iron bearing had been shaken by that unexpected late afternoon meeting.

The commander had not wanted to go at all. There had been a visiting dignitary from Holland, a meeting with the Canadian ambassador, two majors arriving from U.S. Army Intelligence, a hundred urgent papers on his desk, and suddenly this call had come to drop everything and run to an urgent meeting for which Sally had been given no reason whatsoever.

The commander had stormed off, ready to give a solid broadside to whoever was responsible. But he had returned two hours later so troubled that his normal ruddy features had been positively ashen. Sally had risen in alarm at the sight, for some reason pierced by a brilliant shaft of fear. The commander had waved her back into her chair and wordlessly entered his office.

Harry Grisholm arrived thirty seconds later. He was not shaken. He was furious. He stormed through her antechamber without even seeing her, entered the commander's office, and shouted, "What an utter shambles!"

"Lower your voice," the commander rumbled.

"Six months in the making," Grisholm went on, only barely quieter than before. "Delete that. Six months of maneuvering before even the first step could be taken. Then what happens, but we find ourselves faced with the loss of every single American agent NATO Intelligence had in the Soviet sector. But did we suspect something? Of course not. How on earth could we? We're all so naive as to think that those seven villages just happened to have been chosen for relocation. All within twelve weeks of each other."

As quietly as she could manage, Sally scooted her chair into the corner of her office. She was certain that if they realized she was still there they would close the door and close her out. And this she wanted to hear.

"So we send our most senior American operative," Harry went on in barely controlled fury, "the man slated to rise into commanding position, over to pick up two defecting German scientists. A trial run, we call it. A chance to pick up some field experience."

There was the sound of Harry's chair being shoved back so hard it slammed up against the wall near her head. Then the little man began his rapid limping pace. Back and forth, back and forth, the words a furious torrent. "And what do we learn now? That the agents in place were identified and picked up because they were *known* to be agents. Why? Because we, the supposed crown jewel of NATO operations, have been infiltrated by Stalin's henchmen."

Sally heard a faint scratching below her. She glanced down, realized it was the sound of her own fingernails digging through the fabric of her chair, the knuckles white with the strain of not screaming out her fear.

"I feel as though I've taken a direct hit amidships," the commander mumbled.

"And well you should. We all have. Every one of us. Especially that poor fellow we've just sent out without the first hint of warning."

"You think the Soviets know what his mission is?"

"I dare not." The pacing became even swifter. "They must have the same communication delays as us with their agents in the field. They *must*. It would take a certain amount of time to first receive the information, and then act on it, especially as far away from Moscow as Rostock."

Rostock. There was no longer any doubt, despite her every desire to refuse to imagine it really was Jake. Jake. Her Jake was in terrible, terrible danger. Sally sat there, her body stiff with terror, her head slowly shaking back and forth, unable to even draw breath.

The commander sighed. "So what do we do now?"

"There is nothing we *can* do. Not until we are certain where the leak is located."

"I suppose I could go," the commander offered.

"Oh, don't be a total fool," Harry barked. "You're far too well known. As is every other senior officer here, including myself. That's why we're here and not still in the field."

"You're correct, of course," the commander admitted. "But we must do something."

"We can do *nothing* until the leak is isolated," Harry countered. "You know that as well as I."

"Quite right," the commander murmured. "No sense sending even more men out to their doom."

Doom. The word echoed through her being like the tolling of a funeral bell. Her own. For without Jake her life was over. Finished. No longer a life at all.

"Not to mention the fact that we might be sending word to the enemy that we know of their infiltration. If they hear that, they will speed things up, make every effort to seal off his escape." The pacing slowed, halted, the angry voice lowered to a worried mutter. "If he can still escape at all."

Chapter Six

————

I t was the longest afternoon of Sally's life.

She remained brisk and busy, forced herself to stay cheerful and show nothing was wrong as far as she knew, even though inside she died a little with every passing second.

To make matters worse, much worse indeed, she knew she could not give in to panic and desperation and worry. She had to *think*.

The first time the commander happened to leave the office, she called her colleague on the floor above. "Rose? It's Sally." She paused impatiently while the phone chattered in her ear. "Yes, I know. The commander's in a major tizzy down here, too. No, no idea. Listen, I need you to cut me a set of travel documents. No, leave out the name, I haven't heard anything about who yet. Flight tonight to Berlin. Yes, that's right. Tonight. Official pass into the Soviet sector. Leave the names blank, I'll type them in as soon as it's cleared up, then call you back. You're a dear. Thanks. Bye."

When she set down the phone, Sally found that the strain of keeping her tone light and easy had caused her knuckles to squeeze the receiver so hard they had difficulty unlocking.

Another hour of agony, then the commander left a second time. She was up and out of her chair as soon as the outer door closed behind him. Sally bundled up a pile of papers and her shorthand pad, shook her head violently enough to unpin her hair, took a deep breath, and left the room.

She raced up the stairs, arriving on the third floor out of breath and flushed, just as she intended. She tripped down the hallway, casting out hurried smiles and hellos to everyone she passed, knocked on the door, and breezed in immediately, saying, "What a day, what a day, what a day."

The heavyset bespectacled man looked up and drawled in best New England nasal boredom, "Why, Sally, dear. You look positively frazzled."

"Something big is going on, I can feel it." She leaned across the wooden barrier, asked with the gaiety of just another office snoop, "Heard anything?"

"Even if I had, do you think I would tell you?" His head dropped back to the document under his oversized magnifying glass. "You'd just hop back down to the power station and tell some bigwig on me."

"Wendell, dear, you know I'd never do such a thing. Not to you." Wendell Cooper was the operation's forger, his work so good it passed inspection by top experts. Which was the only reason he was tolerated. Those occupying the power station, the name given to the offices on the ground floor, thought him overly effeminate and slightly balmy besides. They avoided him at all costs.

Sally knew Wendell to be both truly lonely and a genuine lover of gossip. He fed voraciously on the little tidbits Sally passed him from time to time and responded with his own brand of friendship. Sally went on in her most excitable manner, "I'm sure something big is going on. I can feel it in my toes."

"You don't say." Wendell pretended boredom. "Well, you'll be sure and tell me what you hear. It helps to pass the hours. Speaking of which, how's the gallant colonel?"

"Off having loads of thrills and adventures," she said brightly, though it cost her dearly to force the words around the lump in her throat. "The lucky stiff."

"Good time to be away, if you ask me. There's the feeling around here that heads may roll."

"Speaking of being away," Sally said, unable to stand it any longer. "I need a passport, please. It's urgent."

Wendell sniffed. "It always is, dear. You'll learn that with time. Getting everybody into a whirlwind gives them a sense of power."

"Maybe so, but I was sent up here by rocket."

Wendell had still not looked up from his work. "Nationality?"

"Swiss."

"A neutral. Hmmm. Must be something very big not to be going with one of our own. Where is he headed?"

"She. I'm not supposed to say," Sally poised delicately, then added the spice. "But I was ordered to have documents prepared for a crossing into eastern Germany."

He looked up at that. "They are sending a woman into the Soviet sector?"

"Strange, isn't it?" She leaned farther across, kicked up one heel as though nothing mattered more than a little gossip. "Wish it could be me."

"No you don't. Not if you want to ever wake up in

your own bed again. Those Russkies play for keeps."
Wendell sighed, pushed his work to one side, opened
a drawer, sorted through a pile, and plucked out a red
passbook emblazoned with a gold seal. He carefully
folded it open on his desk and slid it under the heavy
glass ring, said, "Name?"

Sally gripped the papers to keep her hands from
trembling, pretended to inspect her pad, replied,
"Stella Frank."

A long moment of silence, interrupted only by
Wendell's quiet scratching. "Residence?"

"Parc des Eaux Vives, Geneva."

"Best let me see that, dear, I don't speak a word of
the Frog language."

"What, and try to decipher my chicken-scratch?"
She spelled it out for him, then gave her birthdate and
birthplace.

"We'll give her the standard travel stamps," Wendell said, choosing several from the revolving trays on
his desk, knowing by rote whether blue or red or green
or black ink was required. "Ready with the darling's
photo?"

"Not yet." Sally shrugged at his look of irritation.
"Don't get mad at me. I just salute and serve."

Wendell looked at his clock. Almost five o'clock.
His anger became genuine. "Surely they don't expect
me to sit here all night until the lab is finally ready to
wake up."

Sally pretended concern. "Just let me have the
stamp. I'll glue it in myself, bring everything back tomorrow."

"Thanks ever," he said, clearly relieved. "I wouldn't
mind, but I've already made plans." He handed her the

passport, a circular stamp, and the inkpad. "Top left-hand corner of the photo."

"You're a dear." Sally gathered everything to her breast and gave him a brilliant smile. "Whatever it is you're up to tonight, I hope it's fun." Then she fled.

The travel documents were on her desk when she returned, which almost stopped her heart until she realized that the commander had already left for the day. Sally slid them into the typewriter and filled out the requisite information before her nerves could give out. Her flight was not until eleven-thirty that night. Plenty of time. She sat and pretended to work as the clock crawled through two complete revolutions, the amount she had already decided was the minimum she could risk.

At seven o'clock she grabbed up a few interoffice memos and letters. They would normally be delivered the next morning by the office boy, but they gave her at least a flimsy excuse to do what was clearly the risk-iest part of her preparations. She took a deep breath, willed herself to act both calm and tired, just finishing up another long day. Then she stepped into the hall.

The corridors were silent, save for the occasional guard and janitor. Sally walked from office to office depositing the papers, greeting all she passed, slightly amazed they could not hear her pounding heart.

The door to Harry Grisholm's office was unlocked. She pushed in, crossed to his desk, and stopped, wondering now where to begin.

Then she saw it. There in his file basket. Covered by other papers, but one edge poking out, and on it the name of her beloved. Jake Burnes. His file. Sally's legs almost gave way at her good fortune.

Her fingers shaking uncontrollably, she switched

on Harry Grisholm's desk lamp, opened the file, and read. Because she liked Harry, she had been immensely glad when she heard that he was to be Jake's handler on this case. But nowhere near as elated as now.

It was all there. The contacts, the itinerary, the addresses, the handover, everything. Sally wrote as fast as her quivering hand would permit, certain every moment that the door would open and she would be caught, captured, chained, kept from doing what she knew she had to. Only she. No one else to trust. No one.

She slapped the file shut, hugged it once to her chest, whispered to the dark ceiling, "I'm on my way, darling." Then she was out the door and gone.

The officer of the guard at the main gate did not think there was anything out of the ordinary in Harry Grisholm's nine o'clock return. The little man was well known among the staff for his odd hours. The guard saluted his car, ordered the barrier to be raised, and made a note in the book. He then looked up, only to find the little man waving him over to the car.

"You're Lieutenant Towers, do I have that right?"

"Sir, yes sir," the young man replied, astonished and immensely pleased to be remembered.

"Good, good. I was just wondering, Lieutenant, is anybody working late tonight?"

"Sir, not that I know of, but I could check the book for you."

"No, that won't be necessary. I was just wondering if anybody might still be around."

"I'm pretty sure they've all gone home, sir. Mrs.

Burnes, she was around again late, but she left almost an hour ago."

"I see," he said slowly. "Mrs. Burnes has left, has she?"

"Signed her out myself. The guards are going about their rounds now, but they all know you, sir. I'm sure there won't be any trouble if you need to get back in."

"No, no, not if everyone has already left for the night. Would you mind if I used your phone for a moment?"

"Course not, sir. Right this way." The lieutenant watched the little man pry himself awkwardly from behind the wheel, then limp over to the guardhouse. He could not help but stare. Everybody knew how Harry Grisholm had received his wounds.

Harry picked up the receiver and dialed a number. "Commander Randolf, please." A moment's pause, then, "Edgar. Harry here. I'm in the guardhouse at the main gate. I'm afraid I can't do that memo we discussed after all. Wanted to call you immediately and just let you know it will have to wait until tomorrow. It appears that your diligent assistant has already called it a night. Yes, that's right. She left almost an hour ago, according to the lieutenant here. No, no problem, just thought you should know. Yes. All we can do is wait, I suppose. Until tomorrow then. Goodnight."

Harry Grisholm hung up the phone. "Thank you, Lieutenant. Very good of you."

"No problem, sir. Anything else I can do?"

Harry looked up at the young man and gave that gentle smile from the eyes that warmed the young man to the bone. "Thank you, Lieutenant. I shall remember your kind offer."

"Thank you, sir." The lieutenant held the car door, shut it, saluted smartly as the car turned and went back out into the night. He watched long after the lights had disappeared. This was one for the books. The young man shook his head. It wasn't every day that he had a chance to talk with a living legend.

Chapter Seven

The hours passed with the brutal slowness of waiting for war.

The night was dry and warm and clear, and filled with the music of a forest in full June concert. Jake leaned his back against a pine just outside the perimeter fence, his face and hands blackened, his clothes as dark as the surrounding night. He knew it was useless to try and doze. There had been many in his squads who could drop off at a moment's notice and wake instantly refreshed ten minutes later, alert for the smallest sound even when asleep. But not Jake. Five minutes or five hours, if he slept at all he woke groggy. And tired as he was now, if he managed to doze off he would probably sleep for hours.

But fatigue was a familiar companion, as was the waiting. War had forced him to come to know many such cronies. Liking them had nothing to do with it. To survive meant understanding their ways and using them for his own benefit.

Jake's mind continued to drift back over the war. He found himself thinking of his younger brother, the one who had not returned from the Normandy invasion. Jake had never seen Bobby again after his own departure; all Jake's memories were of the young man before leaving the U.S. Suddenly his brother's fresh and eager face became superimposed over the image of the blond scientist, tall and arrogant and cold and superior. A perfect Aryan Nazi. The enemy. Just like the ones responsible for blasting his last living relative to smithereens. Now here he was, risking his own neck to bring the man out. Jake shook himself like a dog emerging from the water and began refitting his packs. There was no future in thoughts like that.

Strange, though, how being here in this midnight terrain brought him closer to the war than he had been since leaving the Italian battlefields. Nothing in Badenburg or Karlsruhe had affected him like this. Here in the depths of darkness, surrounded by danger, he was beset by memories and sensations which he had thought gone forever, lost both by time and his own acceptance of faith. Yet now he sat and struggled with both the external dangers and the same internal forces of fury and vengeance that once had dominated his existence.

Jake loathed the fact that he was risking his life to save an enemy. And that was how he saw Hans Hechter. No matter that he was needed by Jake's government, that his mind and his knowledge was deemed essential. In the instant of facing the scientist, Jake knew he had come face-to-face with the foe.

Yet there was something more. Jake knew this for a fact, and yet could not come to grips with how he knew or why it bothered him so. He was faced with an internal struggle so deep he could not truly fathom what it was, one which left him feeling unsettled and angry. With Hechter, with himself, with life. Jake was a straightforward kind of person, not given to long introspective battles. This sort of hidden confusion left him very disturbed.

He checked his watch, found himself genuinely glad to be able to focus on something else, even something so dangerous as his present mission. He tightened the straps to his two packs, one gripping his chest and the other his back. He slid the wire cutters from his leg pouch and started forward.

The wire gave him no problem at all. The strands were rusted almost through, the ground unkempt and so weed-infested he could almost have stood upright and remained hidden. Clearly the guards had wasted little concern on keeping up security since the war. Jake folded the two sides of the fence back to form an opening in the shape of an inverted V. As he slipped through, he had the fleeting impression that the wire had been left there more to keep the scientists in than the enemy out.

There were no dogs, only one pair of guards who gave the terrain a haphazard circuit every half hour. Jake had watched and timed and was certain enough of his relative safety to risk a run straight across the concrete launch-pad. The entire perimeter, both of the pad and the complex itself, was ringed with tall poles sprouting lights like multiple steel branches. Yet only a handful still worked, and these flickered and popped so much that they generated more shadows than light.

Jake reached the first set of steel doors, sidled around to where the cliffside was covered with a pelt of uncut grass, and began to climb. The cloudless night was so bright as to faintly wash the cliff and the doors and the fields and distant trees to colorless silver. When he was directly above the doors, he reached into the chest pack and drew out the first bomb.

The bombs he had brought were bulky, heavy, and made to be used by someone who had no knowledge whatsoever of explosives. Anticipating that he would be up against some form of reinforced subterranean compound, the bomb's designers had delicately balanced power with directive force. The intention was to focus the bomb's force inward to where it would hopefully inflict structural damage. The result was a squarish charge fastened to what looked like a heavy metal pie plate, with the timer a sort of afterthought dangling from one end. Jake gave the timer a final check, dug the hole, set the bomb. Then he scrambled down and moved on to the next door.

He set the four bombs, all he could carry, above the four doors closest to the entrance where the scientists were scheduled to be waiting. He scrambled down to ground level, crouched in the shadows of a concrete entrance platform, waited for the guards to pass. The single team talked loudly as they walked, keeping themselves company.

Carefully he skirted around the illuminated islands created by three working light posts. He checked a final time, then climbed the entrance stairs where Hechter and Grunner were to be waiting. The doors were locked. Jake made a swift inspection. Definitely a holdover from the former proprietors. Solid steel construction, bolted directly into the stone framework. Jake extracted his remaining three charges, all much smaller and less powerful than the ones dug into the hillside. He set them as he had been instructed, taping one to the top of the seam made between the two doors, the second at the base of the seam, the third directly over the central lock. He stepped back, desperately hoping he had it right. Otherwise Colonel Jake

Burnes, spymaster extraordinaire, would be left standing there behind enemy lines with not even a butter knife to get the doors open.

Jake did a quick swivel-check of the surroundings and satisfied himself that his work had gone unnoticed. He slid off the platform, crouched down far enough that the concrete landing would act as a buffer, fitted in his earplugs, checked his watch, and prepared to wait.

It was strange how, surrounded on all sides by the night and by danger, his thoughts would turn to Sally. Jake settled into a more comfortable position and decided maybe it wasn't so strange after all.

Theirs was more than a loving relationship, he realized. She had *restored* him. The void caused by the loss of his own family had been filled by his marriage to Sally.

His marriage. The wedding had been a simple affair, held in the Karlsruhe military chapel now run by Chaplain Fox, their friend from the Badenburg relief center. Jake had called in all his chips and wrangled military transport to bring over Sally's parents. Pierre and Jasmyn had been there, along with Lilliana Goss and Kurt and a few military pals. The meager crowd had been vastly augmented by Jake's unbounded joy, so strong that he felt the chapel would burst from trying to hold it all.

Sally had worn a cream-colored wool suit with a pleated skirt and fitted jacket over a white silk blouse. Her hat had been trimmed with a half-veil of lace, as simple and beautiful as her bouquet of roses and wildflowers. Jake had often heard that grooms remember nothing of the ceremony. But not him. The memory of Sally's luminous beauty, and the love which had shone from her eyes, was etched upon his heart for all days.

With his mind so far away, the explosions coming so loud and so close almost stopped his heart.

The three blasts of the door-charges, going off within a heartbeat of each other, sounded like a mad giant hammering a massive anvil and ripping it to shreds in the process.

Jake raised his head above the level of the platform. He was immensely pleased to find the frame and the supporting rocks shattered, the doors bent and smoldering and barely upright.

Then the night was shattered a second time. Sirens shrieked. Voices shouted. A single spotlight switched on, too far around the corner of the cliff to shine upon Jake as he vaulted onto the platform and wrenched open the door, using one of the bomb packs to protect his hands. He searched through the acrid smoke for the two scientists, saw nothing, was momentarily panicked by the fear that he had blasted the wrong door.

Then two familiar faces peeked through the smoke. Jake hissed and motioned frantically for them to move. Together the scientists stepped through the frame.

Jake pointed down into the shadows, opened his mouth to tell them to hide, when an icy voice howled, "Stop! I have you covered! Guards, guards, over here!"

The scientists froze to the spot. Jake hid behind the door, heard footsteps race down the hall, judged the moment the best he could. Then powered by the gallon of adrenaline coursing through his veins, he slammed the door home. It met the oncoming person with a re-sounding thud. Jake unholstered his gun, jerked the door back open, saw it was the cadaverous political officer who had challenged him earlier. The man was out cold.

"They're coming," hissed Grunner.

Jake pushed the two scientists off the platform and into the neighboring darkness. Pleaded silently with the charges to go off on time. Heard the footsteps and the shouts approach and held his own gun at the ready, wondering what good it would do against such odds, ready to try just the same.

The charge set farthest away blasted with light and thunder and a booming, rocking force that caused the earth to shiver and sent a dust cloud rocketing skyward. The footsteps and shouts abruptly veered off.

Then a closer charge blew. Before the dust began raining back to earth, while the spotlight's glare was dimmed to a frustrated grayish tinge, Jake lifted the two scientists and urged them forward with a shouted, "Run!"

Chapter Eight

Her plane was delayed almost six hours.
Sally slept in fits and snatches on a hard
wooden bench under a broken window. The hangar
smelled of oil and diesel fumes and sweat and old cigarette smoke, so Sally was grateful for the fresh air,
even if it bore an early summer chill. Occasionally she
would start awake. Sometimes it was the laughter and
shouts of men playing poker at the hangar's other end.
Sometimes it was her nerves playing tricks with her
dreams, imagining a hand reaching out, grabbing her,
shaking her roughly, telling her it was time to give up,
come back, face charges, go before the tribunal and be
sent to women's pris—

"Mrs. Burnes? Ma'am?"

Sally jerked upright with a squeak. "No! I have to
go!"

"Yes, ma'am." The mechanic wore dirty coveralls
and had a cigarette tucked behind one ear. "That's why
I'm waking you. The plane's ready. We fixed the engine."

Sally rubbed her face, heard the drumming sound
of revving motors, tried to put her mind in order.

"Fixed it so it will stay fixed all the way to Berlin, I hope."

"You bet, ma'am." The mechanic boasted a smile brighter than the dawn. "When the army does something, it does her good."

"You better be right, soldier." She slipped on low heels and used his arm for support as she stood. "I didn't wait this long just to take my morning bath in the North Sea."

"Not a chance, ma'am. More than my life's worth. This plane's got more brass on board than the Pentagon. Something big must be going down in Berlin." He glanced over his shoulder and so missed Sally's fleeting look of alarm. "See the one with all the braid and the stars? He's been giving you the eye. Looks like you're the only dame, I mean lady, on board."

A flash of irritation ignited her heart and lifted it to cruising speed. She managed a genuine smile for that little gift. "Thanks, soldier. I've got a little experience handling guys with more brass than brains."

The mechanic's grin lit up the hangar. "Bet you don't even leave the bones, ma'am. Have a good flight."

Sally stood, checked herself in a window turned into a dark mirror by the predawn gloom. Sensible but smart—that was how she had chosen her clothes, not the way she felt about what she was doing. She was trying to act smart, maybe, but certainly not sensible. Beige silk blouse, cotton skirt one shade darker, light-brown pumps, a single strand of charcoal gray pearls, her only splash of color a bright silk scarf knotted at her neck and draped over one shoulder. Sally patted her hair into place, picked up her brown raincoat and bag, and walked toward the officers milling about the hangar exit.

True to the mechanic's warning, as soon as Sally started forward a light colonel broke off from the general's band and started toward her. He was a picture-book exec, his uniform tailored and hair freshly cut. Sally was certain he had earned all his ribbons driving a desk.

He touched his forehead with a casual smirk of a salute, said, "General Hastings was wondering if you might enjoy a little company on the flight."

"Why don't you ask the general to come on over here himself," Sally replied crisply, continuing to walk toward the exit, "so I can tell him no personally."

The colonel started at her response but recovered quickly. "Now, ma'am," he drawled. "A man like the general could do your husband, whoever he is, a world of good come appointment time. All he's asking is for you to be a little friendly."

"And all I'm asking," Sally retorted, stopping and facing him square on, "is to be left alone. And for your information, Colonel, my husband happens to be a *man*, not a nursemaid to a general's ego." She turned away. "Now, if you'll excuse me, I have a plane to catch."

As she stood in line waiting to board the plane, a voice behind her said, "That's sure telling him."

Sally wheeled about, ready to give someone else the remnants of her anger. But she was met by a rugged face, a cheerful grin, and two outstretched palms. "Easy, ma'am. I was just offering my congratulations. Never did think much of an officer who used his brass as a battering ram."

She inspected his face and found only genuine

friendliness. "I'll probably regret what I just did in the morning, Major. A lot."

"Don't," he assured her. He then pointed at a band of gold encircling his fourth finger. "Now, if you're looking for a traveling companion who's not going to offer you any trouble, I'm about as happily married as you'll ever meet in this crazy world."

"Sounds like the best offer I'm going to hear in what's left of tonight," Sally replied, deciding that here was a fellow she could trust. "Thanks."

It was only when she was inside and searching for a seat that she realized she had forgotten to worry. Sally walked down the crowded aisle, nodded when the major offered her the window, slid into her seat with a sigh. Almost airborne.

The major waited until they were both settled and the motors had begun their takeoff revving to offer her his hand. "Theo Travers."

"Sally Burnes."

"Burnes, Burnes," he rubbed his chin. "I know that name."

"My husband is Colonel Jake Burnes."

The major brightened. "Sure! The Karlsruhe garrison commander, or was. My last posting was in Stuttgart. Hey, is it true what they say about him and the desert crossing and all that Sheik of Araby stuff?"

"I wasn't there," Sally replied, "but he did receive the Croix de Guerre directly from the president of France for what happened."

"Wow." The major shook his head. "Adventures in the back of beyond, then he comes home and gets the girl. How come it only happens to the other guy?"

The plane was old, the soundproofing feeble. The great rumbling engines offered them an island of privacy. "What about you," Sally asked. "What takes you to Berlin?"

"Beats me. I was packing up ready to be shipped home, demob papers tight in my sweaty little grip. Then what happens but I get these urgent orders to strap on my gun and make tracks for Berlin." He rubbed a stubbled chin. "Been traveling almost twelve hours on a truck older than I am, and let me tell you, I could truly use a bed."

Sally kept her smile politely interested. "What do you do?"

"Construction. Real life, too, or I hope so. Been in since forty-three. Specialized in battlements and fortifications through the war, then demolition for the past couple of years. Which makes all this passing strange. I mean, Berlin is about seventy percent destroyed already, so demolition is out, and what do they need fortifications for since the war's over?"

"I'm not sure," Sally said, and dropped her eyes.

When the major did not respond, she raised her head to find him watching her. All humor was gone from his voice and gaze as he said, "You know something."

"I'm not sure," Sally repeated quietly, and studied the man beside her through the takeoff. His was a comfortable, lived-in sort of face, full of strength and integrity, lined with furrows that gathered comfortably into well-practiced lines when he smiled. "Tell me about your wife, Major."

"Call me Theo. I break out in hives when a pretty woman uses my title, especially when I'm this close to being a civilian again."

"Theo, then." Sally found herself liking the man. He had the look of someone who had come to grips with the good and the bad within himself, who was content with both his station and his direction. "Tell me about her."

"Oh, she's a gem." He leaned his head back on the seat. "Three kids, youngest only two when I was called up. Didn't bat an eye—well, no, that's an exaggeration. But she's done well by us, kept me alive in their minds, a tough thing to do when Daddy's gone for two long years. Only visited them once, and when I was back, gosh, I wish you could have seen how she treated me. Not like I was some visitor. No, like the time I was gone didn't matter now that I was back."

"Sounds like a wonderful person," Sally murmured, liking the way his face lit up as he spoke of her.

"Yeah, too good for me, that's for sure." His smile was directed toward someone only he could see. "She must've found it tough, taking up the reins while I was gone and then passing them back, but you'd never know by listening to her."

"What does she do?"

"Teaches high school math. Got a great mind, handles those kids like they're genuine people and not freaks that ought to be locked up until they hit eighteen." He switched his grin over her way. "Sorry to run off at the mouth like that, ma'am. But you got me onto my favorite subject."

"Call me Sally, please."

"Okay, Sally, so what brings you to Berlin?"

Sally liked him and trusted him. It was a decision at heart level, but she genuinely felt that their meeting was a gift. And she needed a friend. Desperately. She sent a prayer winging upward, then let her worry show through. "I have a problem, Theo. A big one."

"Those are the only ones worth talking about."

"And secret," Sally added. "So secret I could get us both shot just talking about it. Really."

He searched her face, asked, "Your husband?"

She nodded slowly. "He's in trouble."

"With the brass?"

"No, that's my department. Jake is, well . . ." She shook her head. "I don't even know where to begin."

"Try the beginning. Always like to set my buildings and my stories on a solid foundation." He glanced at his watch. "Besides, what else have we got to do with the next five hours?"

Chapter Nine

The March of Brandenburg, as the region surrounding Berlin was known, contained more lakes than all the rest of eastern Germany combined. They were mostly small, set in shallow valleys between rolling hills, bordered by scrub and pine, and lined by some of the worst roads Jake had ever traveled. Many of these country lanes had been constructed of sandy shale to begin with, then blown to oblivion by off-target bombs. The larger roads were segmented muddy bogs, the multitude of bomb holes filled by recent rains. Their remaining surfaces were often ground to gravel by the invading Russian tanks and heavy weaponry. In the worst stretches, recent traffic had bypassed the roads entirely, creating parallel tracks over dunes and bushes that Jake negotiated at a crawl.

Dr. Hans Hechter sat beside him, sullen and silent, his well-trimmed blond head hidden beneath an ancient sweat-stained homburg. Dr. Rolf Grunner had been relegated to the back. The lid to the second undercompartment, now emptied of the satchel bombs, remained propped open, the interior padded with blankets and burlap. If there was a risk of discovery, Grunner could swiftly slide in and close the top. There was far less risk of discovery if inspectors found merely a trader and his helper.

The arrogant blond scientist's presence would have been much harder to bear had Jake not been so worried by what he had seen thus far that morning. Their way had crossed a major thoroughfare a little distance back, and despite its bomb-blasted surface, the larger road had been filled with a military convoy. A Soviet convoy.

And it was the contents of the convoy that troubled Jake.

For the second time their road approached a juncture with the thoroughfare. Jake stopped the truck and climbed to the top of the highest hillock in view. He crouched and looked down on what once had been the famous Berlin autobahn. Hitler had built these incredible four-lane highways—roads fit to carry the emperor of what he expected would someday be called the new Rome. Jake scanned the bombed and tank-scarred surface, remembering Harry Grisholm's lessons as he did.

The two weeks he had been given for preparation and briefing had been too full and too short. Jake's two anchors throughout it all had been Harry Grisholm and Sally. At every turn, with every question, Harry had been there, available and ready with the answers. Even to the questions Jake did not know enough to ask.

"Observe," Harry repeated endlessly. "Do not try and sort at first. Nothing will make sense. Everything will seem either too mundane to be noticed or too bizarre to group together. This is inevitable, and although it will improve as you gain more field experience with us, still your first few days on every new assignment will seem a jumble of conflicting impressions."

"So what do I do?"

"Just watch and listen. You are both intelligent and perceptive. People often think one goes automatically with the other, but that is nonsense. The most intelligent people are often the ones who allow themselves to notice only what is in line with their opinions. So go in with no opinions at all. And block nothing out. Prearranged judgments are comfortable barriers, but they are death to genuine learning." Harry gave his patented smile, the one which touched nothing except his eyes. "Also good advice for people seeking to delve honestly into faith, yes?"

Jake nodded, unwilling to let the point go just yet. "But I need something to hold on to."

"All right," Harry conceded. "Most times, there will be concerns beyond your own specific assignment. Your superiors may even be afraid to tell you what they are, because they often battle among themselves over these very same points. Very little in this game is certain, Jake, especially for people who do not go across the line themselves."

This *game.* "Like what sort of questions?"

"Well, we know for certain that Russians are mobilizing large shipments of both men and equipment throughout much of Eastern Europe."

"I've heard about this."

"Of course you have. And you've also heard how some of our high and mighty decision makers think it is exactly as the Russians claim, that they are simply shifting things around, picking up squads and garrisons stranded since the war and consolidating their hold. Others, however, disagree."

Jake inspected his friend's face. "And you're one of them."

"I am concerned," Harry admitted. "Very concerned. Too much is happening at once. There are noises about the Russians wanting to take over all of Berlin. They positively loathe the idea that the Western allies maintain this hold right in the middle of their territory."

"I haven't heard anything about this."

"You will," Harry predicted grimly. "These politicians who think the problem is going to go away merely by talking are laying us open to very grave dangers."

"What sort of dangers?"

"That's what I want you to find out." Harry's gaze had a piercing quality. "Don't go looking for trouble, mind you. But if you can, find out what the Russians are up to. Have a look at things from the other side. See where these men are headed, what kind of equipment they are carting around. Observe. Seek the unexpected. Strive to fit the puzzle together. And above all, take care. You will be utterly alone out there, Jake. As alone as anyone can be in this day and age—surrounded by millions of people, none of whom you can trust."

Jake picked his way back down the steep hillside, only to find Hans Hechter waiting for him with both hands planted firmly on his hips. "Really, Colonel, this is too much. You know perfectly well that your primary objective is to deliver us safely and *swiftly* to the American sector. I order you to end these ridiculous excursions and get on with the business at hand."

Jake stopped in midstride, too dumbfounded to be angry. "You what?"

"You heard me," the scientist snapped. "I command you to forget this nonsense and drive!"

Jake opened his mouth a couple of times, caught between fury and laughter. He settled on, "Get in the truck."

Dr. Hechter started to speak, but something in Jake's eye snagged his attention. With a stifled oath he wheeled about and stomped to his door.

Jake climbed in his side with a long-suffering sigh. It had been like this since they had emerged from the woods the night before. Dr. Grunner was silent and servile and afraid. Dr. Hechter remained a consistent pain in the neck. He had vehemently refused to climb into the secret compartment, claiming it was beneath his station to travel under such conditions. Grunner had defused the situation by offering to remain there throughout the journey.

Jake continued to regret that offer, both because it left him seated next to the former Nazi, and because the atmosphere would probably have been improved had there been a confrontation in that first moment. But because they were less than a half-mile from the guard station, and because Grunner had already climbed into the truck, Jake had let matters lie.

They had driven through the night, or rather Jake had, going east rather than west, headed back toward Berlin. The powers that be had reasoned that the alarm would be sounded for defectors headed directly toward the western sectors. Jake had followed their pointers tracing a line on the wall-sized map and had not objected at the time; why should he, when he had never been there, had no idea what the roads would be like, and had never experienced what it meant to be behind enemy lines, heading farther and farther into unfriendly territory.

He pushed aside his fears and frustrations, and drove on. His mind was gritty from fatigue and strain, his concentration focused more on what he had seen from the hilltop than on the road or his compass. The military markings on the convey had been clearly visible, the contents of the trucks very disturbing. The trucks headed eastward were not laden with troops, as Stalin was claiming in the newspapers. Jake had seen no evidence that there was a withdrawal underway. The eastbound trucks had not carried men at all. They had been loaded to the gills with loot.

Some of the trucks had covers strapped over their bulky burdens. But not others. Jake had seen everything under the sun being carried eastward—great cheese rings stacked with straw for cushioning and insulation, clattering piles of pots and pans beneath a webbing of rope, tools, bleating animals, possessions of every imaginable description. Two trucks had trundled by while Jake watched, each bearing a trio of great chandeliers strung from an overhead bar, thousands of crystals tinkling and shooting rainbows in every direction.

There was no question in Jake's mind whatsoever. The eastern sector of Germany was being systematically looted, stripped to the very bone. Yet he knew from his own experience how desperate was the plight of the German people. How were they to survive the coming winter, much less begin rebuilding, if even more were taken from them?

His musings and his fatigue kept him from spotting the checkpoint until they were almost upon it.

"Into the compartment," Jake hissed. "Quick!"

As he heard the compartment lid click shut, he braked to a halt, trapped on one side by an armored half-track and on the other by a bomb crater so deep the bottom was lost in shadows. Ahead the road curved around the diminishing hill and joined with two other roads—the autobahn, and a second lane packed with refugees.

The sight of refugees struggling along on foot was a familiar sight, but one which he could never grow accustomed to witnessing. Here too was an element of unsettling surprise. He had thought that the flood of refugees had been almost stopped. The camps were established and well run, papers were being organized, food was relatively plentiful. At least, that was the situation as he knew it in the west. Jake stared through the windshield, drawn to the tragedy in front of him despite his own danger, and found himself transported back to the first bleak months following the war's end.

The refugees' faces were drawn taut with exhaustion and hunger. Men, women, and children walked on worn-out shoes, pushing cycles or barrows piled with their earthly belongings, or carrying everything on their backs. Their eyes were nightmarish caverns, blank and empty of hope. They walked, on and on and on, pushed by forces so far beyond their control that their pleas were silenced.

Jake watched a group of Russian soldiers pawing through a family's belongings, fighting over a shawl and laughing uproariously as the old mother clawed at them and begged for its return.

Jake forced his attention back to matters at hand as two men approached his side of the truck. One was dressed in the scratchy brown wool of a Soviet non-com. The other wore a new uniform of Prussian blue, another of the so-called People's Police. This organization, he knew, was in truth becoming a catchall for the ranks of political officers and assistants to their Soviet masters.

Jake nodded a greeting and handed over his greasy papers without waiting to be asked. As nonchalantly as he could, he motioned toward the refugees and inquired, "Where is this lot coming from?"

"Who knows," the political officer sniffed. "All over. Most recently from the station south of Berlin. There's been another outbreak of cholera."

Jake swallowed his bile and with it the retort that if there was cholera, the last thing they needed to be doing was walking.

"What about you, gypsy?" the officer demanded, his voice a permanent sniff. "Where are you coming from?"

"All over as well," Jake replied, his voice as bored as he could make it. The political officer was not a problem. But the Soviet sergeant was another matter entirely. He was dark, with the leathery skin and high cheekbones of a Mongol. He eyes showed a merciless battle-hardened squint, and he watched Jake like a hawk watched its prey. Jake shifted his gaze back to the refugees and intoned, "My life is that of a traveler."

The officer stood on his toes and eyed Jake's assistant, who sat with eyes straight ahead. He compared the picture on the second set of papers with that of the blond man. "You took an unemployed engineer as your assistant?"

"Is that what he was?" Jake tried for mild humor. "I wondered how he learned the fancy words."

"Was he a Nazi?"

"I don't care about the man's politics," Jake replied laconically. "Just whether he can work."

A wail arose from another group of refugees whose paltry belongings were being tossed to the four winds. The officer looked over, snorted his disgust, then handed back Jake's papers. "Let me see what you have."

Jake stepped from the truck, knowing his papers were supposed to keep him from being looted, yet aware that the sergeant with his unwavering gaze was an unknown force. The Russian stood behind the political officer, one hand continually massaging the stock of his rifle.

The political officer's attention remained distracted by the growing uproar from the refugees. He gave the truck's interior a cursory inspection and was about ready to wave Jake onward when the sergeant spoke for the first time. His guttural voice was barely audible over the din, but the officer stiffened, turned toward the other man, started to retort, then changed his mind. "Unload," he ordered Jake.

He could not help but gape. "All of it?"

"Everything." He was clearly as irritated by the order as Jake.

"But that could take an hour," Jake protested. "More. And we have a delivery to make in Berlin. You saw my papers. They—"

"Don't question my orders," the officer snapped. "Get started."

Resigned, Jake kept his eyes from the watchful sergeant and the itchy trigger finger as he walked to the open window and told the blond scientist, "Start unloading the truck."

But before Jake could walk back and lower the rear gate, Hechter had stormed around the truck, stiff and upright angry in his superiority. He raised his chin, looked down at Jake, and snapped, "Now see here, Co—"

Suddenly all the rage and the tension and the fatigue bundled together in his gut, raging through him like a freak ball of static energy. In one continuous motion Jake swept around and landed a single backhanded blow to the side of the blond man's head. The blast was strong enough to lift Hechter up and spin him around and slam him into the side of the truck. He clutched feebly at the canvas as he sank slowly to his knees.

Jake stood over him, his chest heaving, the rage flowing through him like waves. *Colonel.* There they were, surrounded by danger and foes on every side. And still the fool had almost said the word. "Don't you ever question another of my orders," Jake rasped, his voice alien to his own ears. "The war is over. You and your kind lost, engineer. If you want to live, you work. You speak when I tell you to speak. Otherwise you stay silent, and you *obey.*"

Jake waited, aching to have the man stand and try to give him more of that cold superior lip, just try. But the scientist dragged the back of one trembling hand across his face, inspected the blood, and stayed there on his knees.

The rage still roaring in his ears, Jake bent over and with one hand lifted the man as though he were a puppet. His other fist cocked back for a final blow. Hechter cowered, his bloody hand raised in abject defense.

Seeing the man crouch like that drained the fight from Jake. He unclenched his fist, stepped back, and rasped, "Now go unload the truck."

Jake turned around, only to find the sergeant grinning openly. Approval shone from those dark hard eyes. This was something the soldier could understand. Another man who maintained discipline with his fists. The guard nodded once, then stopped Hechter's shaky progress toward the truck's back with the gun barrel. He spoke more of those guttural words, then turned away.

"You may go," the political officer muttered, his own gaze full of cautious confusion.

Jake looked from one to the other, then motioned with his head for Hechter to climb back on board. He then walked to the back of the truck, pulled one of the grain sacks toward him, opened the neck, and stuck one hand inside up to the elbow. He fished out two hidden bottles, retied the neck, then walked over to the soldier.

He held them out, one in each hand, and met the fathomless gaze straight on.

The gap-toothed grin reappeared. "Wodka?"

"The best money can buy," Jake confirmed in German.

The sergeant shouldered his gun and took the bottles, his unshaven face split almost in two. *"Da, da, na zadrovie."*

"Anytime, mate," Jake replied, and started to turn away. But a hand on his arm stopped him. The sergeant shouted to the officer. The officer replied in what was clearly very rusty Russian, but the sergeant was having none of it. He gesticulated angrily with the bottles and roared a command so loud that activity among the ref-

ugees temporarily halted. Then his soldiers saw that
the man's ire was directed elsewhere, and they returned to their looting.

The political officer pulled a sheet of paper from his
pocket, looked at Jake's vehicle tag, scribbled something on it, reached and handed it to Jake, all without
meeting his eyes.

Jake looked dumbly at the paper, then up at the
grinning sergeant. "What is this?"

It took another bark from the sergeant for the officer
to reply, "A Soviet travel permit. Show it to the other
checkpoints between here and Berlin."

Jake nodded his dumbfounded thanks at the sergeant, who toasted Jake with the bottles. He then
turned and bellowed at his soldiers, who left their sort-
ing and began making a way through the flood of refugees. Jake clambered aboard, started his engine, and
drove forward with a final wave to the grinning sergeant.

There was one brief moment when their truck was
completely surrounded by refugees, a slow-moving
river which blocked them from view. One of the men
lifted himself from the morass and approached Jake's
window. Jake recognized him as the husband of the
woman who had lost her shawl. The woman stood beside him, two children clutching her ragged skirt, her
eyes unable to shed any more tears.

Jake intentionally flooded the engine, then turned
to the subdued Hechter and hissed, "Grind the starter.
Do it!"

As the scientist reached across and pulled at the
starter, Jake flipped the back canvas curtain aside,
reached and grabbed and came out with four pairs of
boots. He tossed them to the startled man, signaled

hastily to wait. He turned back, came up with all the remaining eggs and bread and cheese. He handed these down, then opened the glove compartment and pulled out one jar of honey. Dumbfounded, the man looked down at the treasures that had appeared from nowhere to fill his arms, then brought his eyes back up to Jake. Jake saw the miles and the misery in the man's face, nodded once, said quietly, "Go with God." He pumped the choke, the truck motor started and caught, and he drove on, the man's gaze etched onto the surface of his heart.

Chapter Ten

As far as Sally was concerned, postwar Berlin was a driver's worst nightmare, and the lighting only made things worse.

Major Theo Travers had picked her up just before dawn, and they had immediately proceeded to get totally turned around. There were few direction markers save on the thoroughfares used for military traffic, and those they wanted to avoid at all cost, since their desire was to go and return without being noticed any more than necessary.

It had taken Travers the previous day and much of the night to arrange things, and to do so without making the kind of waves that would draw unwelcome attention his way. Sally had stayed put in a run-down civilian hostel in the American sector, the best she could manage given her false Swiss passport.

The first thing Theo said when he picked her up was, "Why Swiss?"

"I wanted a reason for the accent they're going to hear with my first word of German, and Switzerland is filled with all kinds of foreigners," she replied, surveying their transport. "Why a dump truck?"

"I've been thinking," he said, climbing aboard. "A

lot, as a matter of fact. Been quite an experience, hearing those rusty gears grind around."

"Speaking of which," Sally said, wincing as Theo fought the lever into first and lurched away, "I hope this thing gets us where we need to go."

"Get us there and back," Theo assured her. "What's more, it'll supply us with the best alibi I could come up with on short notice." He reached under his seat, came up with a sheaf of papers. "Blank order forms. I need a whale of a lot of sand for making cement. Need myself about, oh, four hundred truckloads. So happens there's two disused pits over in the Soviet sector. You're coming along as my interpreter."

"Smart," Sally agreed. Her glimmer of hope was mirrored by the first faint light of dawn. "Four hundred truckloads?"

"You heard right. But there's no need to be telling them that straight off. Leave a little room for bargaining when it comes down to price. Because we really will be needing the stuff." Theo stopped at a blank intersection rimmed by bombed-out buildings, pulled a compass from his pocket, took a sharp left. "You wouldn't believe what they want built here. A full-size garrison town, and that's just for the American troops. Nothing short-term about this baby. They're in for the duration, and the same goes for the other nationals, far as I've been able to make out."

"But why?"

"Seems Stalin's been making some noises that have the other nations pretty riled up. Uncle Joe's basically come right out and told them that he considers Berlin to be his exclusive bailiwick."

"But that's ridiculous. It goes directly against the terms of the UN agreement."

"Maybe so," Theo agreed. "But a measly piece of paper doesn't appear to mean much to that man. One thing I heard yesterday, over in the Soviet sector they're putting up these big old billboards. Imagine, the whole city's in ruins, especially their part, where there hasn't been much reconstruction going on. Anyway, the only thing they're painting are these wall-sized sheets of propaganda. The billboards are in Russian on top, then German underneath. The German says, 'The Soviet Union Wants Peace.' So does the Russian, only the word they use is *mir*, which means both 'peace' and 'the world'." Theo shook his head. "Gotta hand it to the guy, that's a tricky way to get his point across."

Sally took the opportunity of a stop at another intersection to settle her hand upon Theo's arm and say with all the sincerity she could muster, "You are a genuine godsend."

"Never been called that before, especially not by a pretty lady in distress."

"Well, you certainly have earned the title now. A godsend."

"Shoot." Theo Travers rewarded her with a grand smile. "This is the closest I've ever come to a genuine real-life adventure."

"I don't believe that," Sally said. "Not for an instant. I saw the ribbons on your uniform."

"Aw, in the Corps of Engineers they give those things out to anybody who can pick up the right end of a shovel." He pulled up to another intersection, as grim as the others, and declared, "Okay. The vote's in and the word's definite. We're lost."

"Don't look at me." Sally glanced around, saw nothing but rubble and war-torn remnants of buildings making stark shadows in the growing dawn. "This is as close to battle as I ever want to come."

"The American sector is in the south, from Zehlendorf and Dahlem over to Neukölln," Theo mused aloud. "The British sector runs in the middle of the western side, from Spandau to the Brandenburg Gate. The French are up north, and that address you gave me yesterday is directly across from the Froggies. I had planned on going up through the three western sectors, then jumping over at the last moment."

"Sounds good to me."

"Maybe." Another squint at the compass. "The only problem is, every doggone road I find that's not clogged with rubble is leading us right toward the dividing line."

Sally searched the gloomy bombed-out rubble and found no inspiration, only a growing impatience. "I say let's just go ahead and chance it, then."

"Right." He slammed the truck back into gear and started off. "Nothing like meeting trouble head on."

They drove in silence for another half hour, as the tattered city gradually struggled to awaken to another grim day. Lines appeared outside kitchens and bakeries and swiftly grew to incredible lengths. The people looked as gray and tired and used-up as their clothes.

"Horrible," Sally declared quietly.

"You're not kidding. And this is still the American sector. I hear it's a whole lot worse over on the other side." Theo popped the brakes, then continued forward. "Heads up. There's trouble ahead."

Sally searched the lessening gloom, saw the roadblock and stiffened. As they approached, she forced herself to relax, sit back, unclench her purse. She had every right to be there.

Theo pulled up until he was surrounded on three sides by soldiers, all eying him with the sullen wariness of guards pulling long hours at boring duty. He rolled down the window as two men approached, one wearing a spanking new uniform of Prussian blue, the other well-worn fatigues bearing the red Russian star.

The blue-clad soldier saluted smartly and barked out a command. The Russian eyed Theo with eyes narrowed to slits. The major was dressed in a military windbreaker bearing his rank and insignia. He grinned down at the men. "Don't guess either of you fellows speaks Yank."

"Give me your pass," Sally said. When Theo handed it over, she opened her door, stepped down and walked around to the pair. She handed her passport and Theo's military ID over without being asked and said, "The major is head of a large construction project. He needs to buy materials."

The news was so startling that even the Russian soldier blinked, telling the world that he understood German. But it was the other officer who scoffed, "Americans want to buy materials from the Russian sector? Impossible."

"Sand," Sally replied, locking her legs to keep her knees from shaking. "And he'll pay in dollars. American. Cash."

That brought another shock wave. "Sand we have," the officer admitted reluctantly. "How much?"

"Fifty truckloads to begin with," Sally said, "if the price and quality are right."

"Fifty truckloads of sand?"

"To begin with. More later. A lot more."

The officer looked to the Russian, who jerked his head back toward the guardhouse. The officer barked,

"Stay here," and scuttled away with their passes.

Sally turned back to the truck. "Now we wait."

"Waiting's fine." Theo propped his feet up on the dash, as relaxed-looking as a cat sunning itself, not a care in the world. "If the army taught me one thing, it was how to wait."

But it was tougher on Sally. She paced until the guards' silent eyes drove her back into the truck. There she sat, consumed with worries and fears and impatience, until the warming day and the scene's utter boredom finally drove her to sleep.

The next thing she knew was a gentle shake of her shoulder and the words, "Rise and shine, missie. The world's a-turning, and the brass've done arrived."

Sally clambered upright from her drowsy slump, rubbed at a sudden catch in her neck, and ungummed her tongue from the roof of her mouth. "What time is it?"

"Just gone noon. You've had yourself quite a nap. Must be feeling chipper and ready to take on the world."

Sally opened her door and slipped down to the earth. She did not feel chipper. She felt decidedly worse than she had when she had fallen asleep. She repinned her russet locks and straightened the scarf over them, pulled the lightweight overcoat straight along the hem, and walked around to where the little group of uniformed men stood waiting. As she approached, she had the sudden impression of her mind working only on one cylinder. Her German was suddenly a distant memory. So she made do with a jerky little nod.

A tall man with the face of an undertaker, white and cold and cavernous, gave a thin-lipped smile.

"Nothing in my experience has ever suggested that a spy would fall asleep at a guard station."

"That's what you think we are?" Sally asked, finding her tongue at last. There was one nice thing about her nap. It had left her nerves so numb that her whole body could just as well have been dosed with Novocaine. "Spies in military uniform and driving a dump truck?"

"I admit it does sound a bit preposterous," the tall man agreed.

"More than a bit."

"So tell me, what does an American soldier find interesting about Soviet-held sand?"

"You have two unworked pits in your sector," Sally replied, rubbing at the crick in her neck. "We don't."

"We?"

She waved an impatient hand behind her. Her neck was throbbing. "The Americans. My employers."

The man examined her a moment longer, then consulted with one of the others, who first shrugged, then nodded. The tall man turned back to her. "It is indeed true what you say. And the sand is certainly better here in the east. So tell me, Madame Translator. What is it the Americans intend to build?"

She turned back to where Theo sat looking down on the scene. "They want to know what it is you're building."

"How much did you say we needed?"

"Fifty truckloads." With her back to the group she motioned with her thumb toward the tall man, meaning, he probably speaks English.

Theo gave a single nod in response and replied, "We need to start reconstruction at several sites. From the ground up."

When Sally had translated this, the man responded immediately, as though already granted time to consider and prepare his answer. "Each truck will come and pay in cash. Each will be escorted by my men for safety, and for this you will also pay."

"Safety," Theo snorted at the response. "Tell the gent he can arrange a brass band for escort so long as the *total* price stays in budget. And my budget is seventy bucks a load. As far as payment is of concern, he can get it from the drivers or by carrier pigeon, it's all the same to me."

"He is unsure that his budget will support such escorts," Sally translated. "But he agrees to pay in cash per load."

But the tall man was already flushed with irritation before she spoke. He turned and signaled to where a trio of soldiers on motorcycles stood waiting. He then handed Sally a card and snapped, "You and the officer are to come to my quarters when you have inspected the pits."

"Nothing doing," the major drawled after Sally had translated, still calm and casual. "Site inspection is gonna take us through today, and tomorrow we've got to dig the samples. If the gent wants to get himself involved, he can come meet us out at the pits."

Sally turned to translate, but the tall man had already wheeled about and started back toward his waiting automobile. From behind her a cheerful voice asked, "Did I say something wrong?"

Sally returned a nod for the motorcyclist's salute, walked around to climb back into the truck, said, "I need a transfusion of coffee. Straight to the vein. Forget messing around with the mouth and stomach and all that nonsense."

Theo grinned at her and revved the motor. "Would you just look at the lady. Deals with some high muck-ety-muck, got the power to shoot us right out of the sky. Is she worried? Not a bit. Cool as a cucumber, this one. A real pro."

"Just let me wake up," Sally replied, settling back into her seat. "Then you'll have the pleasure of watching me shriek and climb the walls."

Chapter Eleven

"H ans is alive only because of good luck and two very important factors," the dark-haired scientist was saying quietly. He had told Jake to call him Rolf. With the journey and fatigue his nervousness had gradually worn away. "First, he resigned the Nazi Party the day after Hitler invaded Russia. He did so quietly, and with relative safety because of the project's importance. His actions meant he would never rise to a position of running the project as he should. But Hans is one of those people who are so sure of their own importance that they feel little need of receiving status from others."

They stood at the truck's tailgate, parked in a rubble-strewn lot. The region had once been a middle-class suburb skirting eastern Berlin's outer border. The lot was now a gathering place for black marketeers. There were perhaps three dozen trucks, another dozen or so horse-drawn farm wagons, and twenty or thirty people displaying paltry wares on threadbare carpets or wheelbarrows or from boxes attached to bicycles. The atmosphere was very subdued. Jake was parked to one side, slightly removed from the others. His display of pots and pans and boots brought many stares, but few who even bothered to ask the prices. They seemed to simply accept that such things were beyond their reach.

"Hans resigned in protest of what he called a tragic repeat of Napoleon's mistake," Rolf went on. "But he did not say this openly. So the Russians were able to view this as an endorsement of their Communist cause. Which of course was nothing more than a means of hiding their true reason for letting him live."

Jake found it difficult to watch the faces. They looked so tired, so resigned. This was far worse than anything he had seen in the days leading up to his Karlsruhe departure, and that had been a good half-year before. Unlike the constant banging and working and clearing and rebuilding which turned every city in the American sector into a unending din, here there was silence. Everywhere Jake looked, he saw the war's remnants standing untouched by any sign of reconstruction. The people mirrored this strange vacuum. They did not even bother to meet his eyes. There appeared to be no room for hope, for bargaining, for anything save a tired envy at the wealth he had on display.

He glanced over at Rolf. The neat, nervous scientist was gone, replaced by a hollow-cheeked trader in denim and tattered sweater, his ratty beard flecked with traces of silver. Jake asked, "And what was their real reason?"

"That Hans was truly the brains behind the project's success," Rolf answered. "Not the name, you understand. Not the senior man who wore the medals and met with Hitler and was pictured in the press. The brains. Your people are right to want him."

Despite Jake's best driving and the newly acquired Soviet pass, they had almost not made it to the contact point on time. Driving in and around eastern Berlin had proved more difficult than Jake had thought possible, with numerous streets still blocked by collapsed buildings and a total lack of road signs. He had finally bribed a teenager with a pair of boots, and the youth had sat on the hood of their truck and directed them with hand signals. They had arrived at the market precisely five minutes before the prearranged contact time elapsed.

There was only a one-hour window each afternoon, a condition of working with local contacts from the British secret service. It had been necessary to go outside normal channels, since all their own men had vanished. The British had refused to give details—names, addresses, descriptions—much to Harry Grisholm's chagrin. They had simply stated that if Jake were to appear at such and such a time and place, they would try and make contact. Try. No guarantees.

Jake had parked the truck, gone around to the back, and swiftly built a little barrier of bundles while Rolf had stood guard. He had then opened the compartment's lid, watched as Hans Hechter blinked in the sudden light, and said quietly, "Five minutes. Stretch your legs, but don't raise yourself up too far. If you hear a knocking, lie flat and pull the lid back down."

Hechter had not replied, just lain there rubbing his eyes. His face was bloodied and swollen where Jake had hit him. Jake walked around to the side cannisters, poured water over his handkerchief, and then filled a cup. He brought both back, said, "I'm sorry for having hit you. But you were about to call me colonel and drop us all off the deep end."

Hechter met his eye for the first time since the confrontation. "You are apologizing? To me?"

Jake looked down at the man, found his deflation unsettling. "Five minutes. No more. Then we'll have to set up shop."

Now Jake looked into the truck's shadowy depths and satisfied himself that Hechter was both hidden and silent. "What about you, Rolf?"

"Ignition and fuel, those are my specialties," he replied quietly, his eyes also scanning the crowd. "Important, but not crucial. I am the equivalent of a five years' advantage, if you see what I mean. Hans, though, he represents a *lifetime*. A full generation's difference in rocket technology to whoever controls that remarkable brain."

Jake looked out over the crowd, glanced at his watch, resigned himself to a night in the open and another day of waiting and hoping. "So why didn't he stay?"

"Resigning the party does not erase the reason for his having joined in the first place," Rolf answered. "The Communists who were put in control of our project need him, but they loathe him as well. Given half a chance, they would execute him on the spot. To make matters worse, we were told in no uncertain terms that we were soon to be relocated to the wilds of Siberia."

Their conversation was cut short as a pair of heavy, bearded men lumbered over. Jake straightened from his slouch and stepped one pace from the truck. Granting himself a little extra room in case the swinging started. Their presence shouted danger.

The taller of the two had one eye turned milky. He had allowed his beard to grow up and cover most of that cheek in a vague attempt to hide a ferocious scar. He reached forward and picked up one of the pans. "Nice wares. From the West?"

"Let's see your money," Jake said, "and I'll tell you all the stories you've got time to hear."

"No, stranger, let's see *yours*," the man said, hefting the pan like a weapon while his shorter companion, a barrel-chested man with the battered face of a barroom brawler, took a step toward Rolf. "There's a charge for displaying your wares here. We're the collection committee."

Jake stood his ground and replied in German, "You can try to make me pay. But it'll probably cost you your other eye."

The tension crackling between the two men was enough to push the crowd of would-be shoppers far away. All eyes were suddenly elsewhere, all attention focused on something safe. The taller man glanced about, then cast the pan back on the tailgate and said quietly, "You do that well for a Yank. Maybe you should consider a different profession."

Jake had difficulty shifting from one danger to the other. "What?"

"Hand me some bills. There are eyes on us. Did you know you were being observed?"

Jake fumbled in his pocket, came up with a handful, passed it over unseen. "No."

"The Soviet minions are paid to check everything new. Yet it appears you two are attracting more than your share of attention." He stuffed the bills in his pocket, pointed with his head. "There is something else. Another stranger. This one's clearly from the West. Been hovering around the outskirts of the market for almost an hour, stopped twice by the police, checked, then let go. Red passport, probably Swiss. You expecting anybody?"

"Not that I was told," Jake said, totally confused by too much too fast.

The big man put a casual hand the size of a bear paw on Jake's shoulder, turned him about. "Let's take a little stroll, I'll just be showing the new man around, pointing out where he's going to be setting up tomorrow." Together they walked down the lot, the crowd parting in fearful waves before them. The man pointed into an empty space between two other metal traders. Jake responded with a single nod. Then as they turned back, the man directed his eyes with pressure on his shoulder, said softly, "There. Beside the curb with the two coppers eying her. In the scarf and macintosh."

Jake felt a blow so strong it whooshed the breath from his lungs. He stumbled as the hand continued to turn him around, managed to whisper, "That's my *wife*."

By the time they had returned to the truck the big man had recovered sufficiently to say, "Something is wrong."

"I'll say." Jake still found it difficult to believe what his eyes had shown him. "How—"

"No time," the man said, and signaled for his companion to join him with a jerk of his head. "I cannot be seen to talk more with you than normal, not until I know what is happening. Traders camp here at night until their wares are sold. Join them. At the far end is the corner of a destroyed building. Back up close and you will be protected from whatever the night brings. Perhaps. There is a working faucet and public facilities two blocks north."

Jake felt as though all the world could see through his subterfuge. "Can we still make it work?"

"We must, though I know not how. The situation has become critical." The big man gave a casual glance over his territory, stretched and said without moving his lips, "My other contacts have vanished, and I have information. Something vital. You must carry it out. How we can accomplish this, with security and spies tightening the net around this place, I do not know. But we must try." He turned, signaled his companion, and stomped away.

Jake stood immersed in confusion and the sense that his carefully constructed world was unraveling. Sally. Here. Part of him wanted to rush to her side. The other part shrieked danger.

The silent clarion grew more strident as he spotted her drifting along with the crowd, allowing herself to be brought along with no sense of her own volition. At each stall she hesitated, picked up an item, set it down, then allowed the shoppers to herd her along. Jake inspected her face, still hardly able to believe it was her. She looked tired. And drawn. Taut to the point that her face held masklike tension. He realized he was staring, felt unseen eyes watching, did the only thing he could, although it tore at his heart to do so.

He turned away.

Jake busied himself with his wares, restacking the pans, pulling bundles about, feeling her draw closer. Then she was there. Standing beside him, close enough that he could smell her scent, feel her presence, and the aching fear and confusion threatened to engulf him.

Sally picked up a pan, inspected it with unseeing eyes. Jake opened a sack, felt inside as though the search occupied all his attention, realized she was holding the pan clenched so tightly her knuckles were white. With the faintest tremor she set the pan back down, and in doing so allowed a slip of paper to fall between the one she held and the one beneath.

She turned away, never having looked in his direction, and as she did so there came a whisper so soft it was almost lost among the crowd's murmuring and the shuffled steps and the gentle evening wind.

"Oh, my Jake."

Chapter Twelve

Firelight sent lingering fingers of light and shadow over their meager campsite. The ruins which formed three sides of their shelter came to life, weaving a silent warning against the debacle of war. Jake sat surrounded by his worries, the note from Sally dangling from his numb fingers, the words read so often that they danced and flickered in his mind.

The scrap of paper looked as though it had been hastily scrawled as she walked. It read simply, "Bären Sand Pits, end of Bärenstr, two km west, 9:00 tom am. Urgent."

Sally. She was here. Everything else paled before the confusion caused by this fact. Was their cover blown? Was that why the nameless one-eyed giant had said there were unwelcome eyes? Jake watched the fire's sparks rise to form glowing copies of the stars and decided that they were probably safe for the night. If the Soviets had wanted to pick them up, they would have done so already. So what to do?

He glanced at his two companions. Hechter had crawled down from the truck, eaten dinner, and now sat staring at the fire without saying a word. They were utterly sealed from the other traders, the truck pulled in close to form the roofless building's fourth wall. Rolf Grunner lay silent and still in his bedroll alongside the truck.

Hechter stirred and rose and slid another rotten plank onto the fire. "I was thinking about the Depression," he said quietly. "No, that is not entirely true. I was thinking of who I am, what I have done, and how the Depression helped to form me."

Jake watched the scientist sit back down. All he had to do was look in the man's direction to feel the hostility well back up. He disliked Hechter on a level far below thought. "Why are you telling me this?"

"Because you apologized," Hechter replied. His voice was as subdued as his eyes. "I have been thinking about that too, Colonel. I have been forced to realize things that I do not like to see, have not wanted to accept. Such as the fact that, for me, power and authority has always meant the right to do whatever I deemed correct. Apologies were not a part of this. I am sure this must seem a minor thing to you. But to me it represents the changes my world is undergoing. And I find myself being confronted with something I have always hated, change."

"So." Despite his hostile feelings, Jake found the conversation a welcome shift from the questions whirling about in his head. "You were saying about the Depression?"

"Nothing you Americans experienced could compare with what happened to Germany in the twenties and early thirties. I know you think I am exaggerating, but I promise you it is not so. Let me tell you just one story, Colonel. My father was a professor of physics at the University of Leipzig, one of the finest schools in the country. I used to go and meet him on Friday afternoons. He would receive his pay, and we would stop by a little cafe where I would have an ice cream and he would sit and drink a real coffee and smoke his pipe. That pipe and his one coffee each week were his only indulgences. We would always take a table far from the windows, so that we did not have to watch the beggars parade back and forth on the street outside. There were beggars everywhere. The women and children were by far the worst, pleading for pennies and clutching at your clothes and screaming obscenities if you did not pay."

He sighed and leaned back against the wall alongside Jake, more than the flickering fire streaking his face with shadows. "For you to understand what I am saying, I must tell you that at the end of the First World War, Germany signed a treaty which forced us to pay money to the victorious nations, especially France. I am not going to argue right and wrong with you, Colonel. All I will tell you is that we were forced to pay money which we did not have. The result was not only a depression like you Americans knew in the thirties, but depression and inflation at the same time. Such inflation as you cannot fathom. So what I describe to you was not happening just in Leipzig, but all over Germany. And it was growing worse on a monthly basis, even weekly."

The call of a night bird brought Jake to his feet. He quietly stalked their perimeter, climbed over the truck, peered out into the shadows and listened carefully. Satisfied, he returned to his place by the fire. "Go ahead."

"Is this hard for you, Colonel?"

"Is what hard?"

"Does it trouble you to hear that the enemy might have had a reason for its actions?"

"There are no excuses for what you people did," Jake said, his voice grating. "None."

There was a long moment's silence, then he sighed, "No, despite my desire to argue and battle, I agree. There was no excuse."

There was a stirring from the bedroll across the fire. A dark tousled head rose to enquire, "Do my ears deceive me?"

"I have always prided myself on my intellect," Hechter replied. "I cannot continue to do so and yet ignore what lies all around me."

Rolf looked from Jake to Hechter and back again. "Wonder of wonders."

"The war was wrong," Hechter went on, his eyes hidden within shadows of two caves carved from years of banked-up exhaustion. "The camps . . . have you seen a camp, Colonel?"

"Survivors," Jake replied, remembering faces behind the wires of the Allied internment camp at Badenburg. "I never want to see any more."

"No, nor I. I have received a letter from a colleague, a man who was employed by the research division of a Bavarian company. He worked in a village called Dachau. He wrote to say that when the Americans arrived, they forced the entire village to walk through the concentration camp outside town. He told me that he did not think he would ever sleep well again. Not ever."

"You mean he didn't have any idea what was going on before?" Jake snorted his disbelief. "You've got to be kidding."

"Of course he knew," Hechter replied impatiently. "We all knew. We all had heard stories of places where in wintertime the sky would rain a white ash that would lay inches thick in the roads. But we all chose to turn away. Not to see. Not to believe that our beloved Fatherland had truly sunk to this level. Such things were unthinkable. They could not be. They could not. They..."

The man could not go on. He turned and stared out over the ruined building, the wall's jagged edge pointing like wounded fingers toward a star-studded sky. He searched the heavens in silent appeal. Then he lowered his face and sighed at the ground, shaking his head slowly, his eyes showing haunted depths.

Jake glanced across the fire to where Rolf now sat and took in the scene with silent caution. Jake found himself agreeing with the man's calculating watchfulness. This change in Hans Hechter was too startling to easily believe. But Jake did not want to let the moment pass. Not yet. "You were going to tell me a story."

Hechter started, as though drawn from a nightmare, and turned his way. "You truly want to hear this?"

Jake nodded, his eyes watchful, unable to commit himself more than that.

"Very well," Hechter said, and straightened his shoulders with visible effort. "I agree that the war was wrong. But it is hard to see where the first step of a new turning will take you. All we knew when the Nazis swept into power was that a firm hand was finally restoring us to a semblance of order. After ten years of growing chaos, this was a tremendous achievement. And remember, Colonel, I am speaking to you as one of the privileged classes. I cannot myself imagine how it must have been for those whose families were worse off."

"Horrible," Rolf said quietly. "My father was an

electrician. There were weeks, months even, when we honestly did not know if we would survive. All I remember of two entire years is a constant, raging hunger. And anger."

"The whole nation was angry," Hechter said quietly. "Even to a child that mood was clear. We had been beaten to our knees, and then beaten again. I myself had not fought in the Great War, and neither had my father. Why was I being forced to pay and pay and pay? I hated all those who had done this to me. Americans and Frenchmen and Russians and all the others, they were just names to me, but names to hate."

"It was easy to hate then," Rolf admitted. "The Communists were the first to use that hatred. The Nazis came later and mixed fury with patriotism, a mixture which proved too heady for some." Rolf stopped, as though waiting for an explosion from his companion. When none came, he raised questioning eyebrows at Jake, but said only, "The Communists were specialists at weaving spells with the magic of rage. That is why I did not join them. I was tempted by their ideals, there was much that they said which I agreed with. But I was frightened by how everything was woven together, not with brotherhood as they said, but with hatred."

"But there were many who did join," Hechter said. "Many. And the anarchists were gathering together many others who hated even more than the Communists, who hated so much that they could not believe in any government. By my tenth year, I had learned never to walk along a main boulevard after school by myself, because several times a week they would be overrun by marches, and the marches always ended up in running street battles. Always."

"The Weimar government was a sham," Rolf offered from his place across the fire. "They had no response to any of the people's demands except the barrel of a gun. The streets of almost every city in the nation ran red with the blood of people who called themselves patriots and whom the government banned as dissidents or criminals or traitors. It was an evil time."

"Especially for a child," Hechter agreed. "I remember one Friday, I believe I was twelve by then. My father came out of the university office, and he was carrying two great sacks, one in each hand. I ran up to him and asked what he had. 'My salary,' he said, handing me one. 'Come, we must hurry.'

"The sack was not heavy, but it was very bulky. Inside were stacks and stacks of bills. I wanted to ask him about this, but he was rushing ahead. My father seldom hurried anywhere. To see him run like this troubled me more than the sacks of money.

"Soon I saw why we were hurrying. I stopped to pull up my socks and saw that behind us was a crowd of other people, all carrying sacks, and all running in the same direction as us. I raced to catch up with my father, truly frightened now.

"Just then we crossed the first main thoroughfare leading to the center of the city, and there was a riot. Policemen and soldiers were shooting at a great mob of people carrying banners for bread. I remember reading that one word, bread. My father always avoided these scenes, especially when I was there. That time he simply cried, 'Not this too! Why do they have to riot on Fridays?'

"He gripped my shoulder, and together we skirted the worst of the fighting, then ran across the street.

Only then did I realize we were headed for the market district. I glanced behind me and saw that all the others were racing along behind us. One man, somebody I knew vaguely because he worked in the same department as my father, was caught by a policeman's truncheon and went down hard. All the others, people he had worked with for years and years, simply raced over and around him.

"My father stopped in front of the butcher's, reached inside my sack, and transferred two great handfuls of notes to his own bag. Then he turned me around and shouted, 'Go to the baker. Buy all the bread you can with that. Don't come outside. Wait for me there. Now run!' I ran.

"There was already a line when I arrived, but not long. Beggars were working the lines as they always did, and I hugged the sack with both arms, ready to kick anyone who came close. But today their plea was different. I came to hear it a lot in the coming days, but this was the first time, and it gave me nightmares. 'A crust, a crust for my babies,' they cried. 'Remember me when you come out.' They did not want my money. They wanted *bread*.

"When it came to be my turn, I did not need to say anything. There was a sign above the counter, with a number bigger than I had ever seen, and just as I was to be served someone came rushing in the door. I was shoved to one side as the sweating baker and his helper started handing one great sack after another over the counter. I was very worried that perhaps they would run out of bread with such an order, but then I realized it was only money. The man shouted something to the baker, who took a thick pencil and added another zero to the giant number on the placard. I realized then it was the price of bread, and it had gone up by another *ten times* just while I was standing in line.

"I bought my bread. It almost filled the sack the money had been in. Then I stood at the far corner and waited for my father to arrive. People were carrying their money in almost everything—knapsacks, bulging briefcases, even a couple of wheelbarrows. Every few minutes the runner would come back, collect the money, and another zero or two would be added to the price of bread."

"Hyperinflation," Rolf said quietly. "It is one thing to hear the word and another thing entirely to try and survive it. Toward the end, when inflation was running at over a hundred percent an hour, my father would insist on being paid before he started a job. My mother would collect the money each morning and race to the shops because by evening his pay was worth half what it had been that morning."

"So you see, Colonel," Hechter said tiredly, "when Hitler arrived and began establishing order, there were many sane and intelligent people who thought the Nazis were saviors, not villains. I was one of them."

Jake stared at the scientist, wondering at all he had heard. Wondering also why his own heart remained so hardened. "And now?"

"Now. Yes, now." Hechter's body had gradually collapsed in upon itself. "How hard it is to admit that my entire life has been built around a lie. Does that give you satisfaction, Colonel, to hear me admit that I was wrong, that I have been wrong for fifteen years, that my entire life has been wasted propping up an evil lie?"

Chapter Thirteen

The next morning found Jake making the hardest decision of his life.

"I can't go," he told the others quietly. "It is one thing to have an assistant who takes off for a while with a friend. If we're being watched, though, and they see me do something strange, they may stop me from coming back. And this marketplace is the only point of contact I have for the man who met us yesterday."

He looked from one to the other, willing them to object, to demand that he come with them. "You've seen her note. I don't know why she's there, or what she can do for us."

"She will be expecting you," Rolf said doubtfully.

"I know." Jake sighed into his coffee cup, watched a glorious dawn turn faded and dismal as it rose over the ruins of what had once been the national capital. From his position leaning on the side of the truck, Jake looked out over an endless display of destruction. Those buildings which remained intact showed sightless eyes to the rubbled streets, their windows boarded over, their doors often barricaded. Jake reached into his pocket and handed over a folded paper. "I have written her a note. It explains that we are supposed to meet our contact here today, that he had something urgent to tell me. Something vital. Those were his words."

"But what—"

"If she can take you through the border, go," Jake said. "That was my first objective, getting you to safety."

Rolf and Hans exchanged glances. "How will you know if we get through?"

"I won't," Jake said grimly. "But that can't be helped. If there's something *vital* that man with the bad eye needs to tell me, then I have to wait. I have no choice."

The smell of coffee and frying bread drifted from one of the early morning stalls. Across the open space came the sound of footsteps scuffling over the rubble. Jake watched the first patrons scurry toward the traders selling black-market food. "She said nine o'clock. You need to get there early, hide yourselves well. Make sure there is no one observing. If there is, wait until she moves toward you, don't go to her." He glanced back at them, nodded once, ached with the desire to go with them. "Good luck."

Theo's first words to Sally when he stopped to pick her up in front of her hostel that next morning were, "Something's wrong."

She felt her stomach zoom down below street level. "You can't go?"

"Of course I can go. Who said anything about not going? I said something is wrong."

She reached up for the side railing and climbed on board, then shut her door. "Theo Travers, you are about to catch some of what has been called my bad side."

He grinned. "A kitten like you?"

She started to snap, then realized there was a worry there beneath his smile of greeting. "What's the matter?"

His smile disappeared. "Easier to show than tell. Let's get started."

Their way took them back along the Kurfurstendamm. Even in the early morning, she saw signs of the growing difference between the city's eastern and western sectors. There was activity here in the west. Makeshift signs decorated the few buildings still intact, advertising everything from clothing to cooking oil. Besides the trundling military carriers, a number of antiquated private cars and trucks puttered about, most loaded to the gills with wares of one kind or another. The people she saw looked tired, but they lacked the haggard hopelessness of those in the east. There was a sense of purpose to their step, an awareness of having somewhere to go.

"It all looks the same to me," she said.

"No it doesn't," Theo replied, and pointed through the windshield. "Up there. Tell me what you see."

She peered, decided, "A police jeep."

"Right. Only the Russkies aren't there anymore." Theo watched the jeep pass before continuing, "I'm quartered over near one of the border crossings. Only place they could put us on short notice. Last night all the Russkies just up and vanished. Not a word. Just weren't there."

Sally felt her nerves draw to humming tautness. "So?"

"So all military police, vehicles and borders and

foot patrols, *all* of them are supposed to have one guy from each of the four sectors. That's part of the plan, see. Four sectors, one city. Only the Russkies have all disappeared."

A sense of foreboding tolled deep within her. "What does it mean?"

"I wish I knew." He rubbed the stubble on his chin. "From what I saw around HQ this morning, it's got some others worried. It's been bad ever since they started erecting their border checkpoints here in the city. That was strictly against regs. But this is something more. This morning the brass were scurrying around like somebody stepped on their anthill."

"Did they make problems about you going over?"

"Naw." The now-familiar grin returned. "Those guys, they know as much about construction as I do about brain surgery. I gave them a song and dance, got them eating out of my hand. Told them how this sand is tons better, which it is, and heaps cheaper, which it oughtta be if those political joes'd get their thumbs out. Never knew buying a few loads of sand could be so much trouble."

Their day yesterday at the site had been almost as frustrating as Sally's trip to the market. A long line of suspicious political officers and their Russian counterparts had come by, each insisting on beginning the negotiations over from the start. Theo had handled it with remarkable calm.

"Heads up," Theo said. "Border check."

Instead of being passed through the American side as was customary, the guard-sergeant stepped in front of the barrier and waved them to a halt. He walked around to Theo's window and saluted. "You Major Travers?"

"The one and only. What can I do for you?"

"Got a call from HQ. Told us to have a jeep escort you over."

"That won't be necessary, soldier."

"It wasn't a request, sir. Orders came straight from General Collins. If they aren't let through, you can't go, sir."

"Eating right out of your hand," Sally muttered. "Better watch out or they might decide to take a couple of fingers."

Theo ignored her, kept his head stuck out the window. "Are my eyes deceiving me, or have the Russkies moved their border station?"

"Yessir. Been at it almost all night. Pushed it back a coupla hundred feet or so."

Theo opened his door and stepped onto the running board. "That a tank?"

"Looks like one to me." The sergeant looked up at him. "You sure you need to be going over there this morning, sir?"

"I'm sure." Theo climbed back on board and shut his door. "Round up your men, sergeant. Let's go see what they're up to."

"If you say so, sir." The sergeant signaled to a waiting jeep, then turned back and said, "Just make sure my buddies all get back in one piece, will you, sir?"

"Right." Theo edged the big truck forward, muttered to Sally, "Stranger and stranger."

The Russian border post had been transformed. Barriers formed from rail cross-ties had been erected in a long forbidding line, with strands of barbed wire strung between them. The long, ominous snout of a tank poked out from a tent of camouflage netting. Armed men were everywhere.

Their arrival was met by a phalanx of stern-faced soldiers with guns at the ready. The same political officer as the morning before came around, saluted them nervously, demanded, "Why are you traveling with an armed escort?"

Sally leaned across and retorted, "Why did you move the guard station? And why the tank?"

The officer reddened. "I will ask the questions here!"

A hand signal from Travers caused Sally to back down. "We have no choice. The major's superior has commanded us either to travel with guards or not to travel at all." She saw the man hesitate, and she pleaded, "We are very interested in beginning these shipments this afternoon. The major has received authorization for immediate payment."

Once again, the offer of dollars softened the man's resolve. "Wait here," he snapped.

He was gone almost an hour before returning and announcing, "There has been a change of plans. The materials will be transported on our trucks. You will pay the costs, of course."

"Of course," Sally said, and turned to translate.

"Tell the guy he can bring it to us by Chinese sampan if the price is right," Travers responded. "But I still need to go collect those samples and talk to the guy responsible for the dig. So how about letting us get out from under the eye of that big gun."

They were eventually let through, but only after they were joined by two Soviet jeeps. Their extended convoy made its way through streets void of life. Sally watched as one boulevard after another appeared, devoid of even the first glimmers of activity. "Something's really wrong."

Travers looked over at her. "We got a squad of Russkies in front and behind us, we've spent the best part of an hour staring down the business end of a tank barrel, and you're just figuring that out?"

Sally met his gaze straight on. "Why didn't you tell me you spoke German?" She watched his double take give swiftly over to a denial, but she cut him off with, "Don't even try, Theo. You knew what I had said to that turkey in blue, and I never even got around to translating."

Travers eased off and grinned ruefully. "Harry told me you were a fast one. Guess I just didn't understand how fast."

It was her turn to play dumb. "Harry? You know Harry Grisholm?"

"Old buddies," Theo affirmed. "Somehow he heard I was coming over. Asked me to keep an eye on you."

"But how—" Sally stopped, the bits and pieces clicking into place. "They left the door to their office open on purpose." And the file. No confidential file would have been left out for the evening, especially not if there was the possibility of a leak. "I've been played for a fool."

"Don't think that even for a minute," Theo retorted. "You were Harry's only hope. Of course, that's all unofficial. Officially, he's hopping mad over you disappearing without a by-your-leave." Theo eyed her with mock seriousness. "Not to mention something about a false passport and illegal travel documents."

"So he told you everything?"

"Not me," Theo assured her. "That's basically all Harry said when we talked, and I got the impression I couldn't ask anything more than that. Which was why

I didn't have to play interested when you spilled the beans in the plane."

She looked at him with suspicion. "Are you a spy?"

"Not a chance," Theo replied cheerfully. "Just watched from the sidelines, is all. Which I guess is why Harry felt like he could trust me."

Sally turned her attention back to the window, her mind churning. The morning was strong and clear, the sky pristine blue. But nothing was stirring. No cars, no people, nothing. "I don't like this."

"Too quiet," he agreed. "Like the calm before the storm. A big one."

The atmosphere of buried tension and fear stayed with them throughout the remainder of their trip. The sand pits were at the end of a lower-class neighborhood whose low-slung apartment buildings extended almost to the company's rusted gates. They drove past the derelict office building, its myriad of broken windows staring down on them like sightless eyes. Two giant mixing towers had escaped the bombings, two others looked as though a giant's hand had crumpled them.

Beneath the last of the towers clustered a group of men who made no move as the convoy pulled up. Beside them waited a long, low sedan painted army brown with a single red star on its portal. As Theo and Sally's convoy halted by the first dig, a soldier opened the car's rear door. A Soviet officer emerged, straightened his tunic, and walked toward them.

"Stranger and stranger," Theo muttered. "What's a Russian officer want with somebody buying a load of sand?"

Sally opened her door and stepped forward to greet the officer, but he ignored her and walked directly to

Theo's side of the truck. In heavily accented but un-
derstandable English he said, "You are Major . . ." He
paused to inspect a card in his palm. "Major Travers?"

"That's me." Theo opened his door and slipped
down. "What can I do for you?"

The officer's eyes were as glacial as his voice. "Your
papers."

"Sure." His cool unruffled by the officer, Theo
handed over his military ID. "Mind telling me what
gives?"

Instead of replying, the officer gave Theo's pass a
minute inspection, then turned and snapped his fingers once in the direction of the waiting group. Instantly one older man doffed his cap and came scurrying over. "Ja, Herr Oberst?"

The officer acknowledged Sally's existence for the
first time. "You will tell this man that he is to execute
the major's instructions, so long as they are restricted
to digging in the pits here within the compound perimeter. You will tell him that the major is to pay for his
services. Is that not correct, Major?"

"Anything you say," Theo replied with false ease.

"Trucks will begin making delivery in four days,
unless there are . . . delays." A hint of a smile appeared,
then vanished without a trace. "You will pay seventy
dollars for each load. Cash. No negotiations."

"Seventy it is," Theo agreed.

The officer glanced at his watch. "I was informed
that you require samples."

Theo gestured toward the truck. "Got the shovels
and the sacks in the back."

"You are to gather your samples and depart before
twelve noon." He fastened his full attention upon the
major. "You will not be permitted to delay your de-

parture one minute beyond twelve. Is that clear?"

"Twelve sounds good to me."

"I don't care how it sounds, Major," the officer snapped. "I am telling you what you will do. You will treat these as orders, and you will obey. Now is that clear?"

Instead of anger, there was merely a deepening to Travers' gaze. Even from where Sally stood, she could see the depth and strength beneath the major's calm veneer. All he said was, "Perfectly."

Without another word, the officer wheeled about and stomped away. He stopped to give crisp orders to the two jeeps, then walked back to his car. The driver closed the door behind him, climbed in and shut his own door, then drove off.

Travers watched them depart in thoughtful silence. Then he turned to examine the old man who stood waiting to one side, his hands crumpling the brim to his battered hat. "Ask the fellow here what's planned for this afternoon. And why the streets here have about as much life to them today as a tomb."

When Sally had finished translating, the man nervously replied, "I know nothing, madam. Nothing at all. I am a simple laborer. My family is hungry. I will work hard. Please, tell us what it is we are to do."

"It's like trying to get an answer out of a rabbit," Sally told the major.

"Well, he's had a lot of experience in learning how to survive." He raised his hand toward the old man, motioning for him to stay where he was, then grasped her arm and led her toward the first sand pit. More quietly he asked, "See the good Colonel Burnes around here anywhere?"

"No." She squinted in the growing sunlight,

searched the empty grounds, willed him to appear before her eyes, for them to get back in the truck and
leave and have all this behind them for good. "Not a
sign."

"With our minders over there, I'm not surprised."
Theo motioned toward the bottom of the pit. "Okay,
then let's make a little circuit, just the two of us. I'll
point out places and afterwards you go back and tell
them where they're supposed to dig. A sack from each.
Got that?"

"Yes." They were so close. If he got her message. If
he wasn't picked up. If, if, if. Her legs suddenly felt
weak as water.

"Steady, now." They made a slow circuit of the first
pit, started over the uneven ground toward the second
hole. Beyond was a pile of dirt excavated and mixed
and ready for shipment. It had rested there long
enough to sprout a meager crop of weeds. Beyond it
rose a motley-colored sand dune with a giant hunk bit-
ten from the nearest face. Theo led her slowly but
steadily in that direction, pointing every once in a
while, Sally nodding with one hand pressed to her
chest, certain that if she did not keep a solid grip her
heart would leap from her body.

"Maybe he's worried about me," Theo muttered.
"Guy doesn't know me from Adam. Okay, let's split up
here, you walk over that way, keep your eye on me. I'll
make little motions, you mark spots with your foot."

Sally moved off and headed toward the hillside.
And even though she was waiting for it, eager for it,
hoping with all her heart for it, when the hiss came
from the little channel she was about to cross, she al-

most collapsed with fright. She recovered quickly enough to make it look like a stumble, returned Theo's signal, stood and looked across the pit toward the major, and whispered, "Jake?"

Chapter Fourteen

The pan he was just about to stack slipped from his hand, rattled on the tailgate, then clanged on the rocks below when the voice announced, "Your wife is a very beautiful woman."

Jake did not need to look to know it was Hans Hechter. "Where is Rolf?"

"Gone." He kept his voice low as he bent over, picked up the pan, and wiped it with his grimy handkerchief. "She is intelligent as well. Not to mention courageous."

"Gone where?"

"To the American base. Disguised as a sack of sand, riding in the back of a dump truck, escorted by two jeeploads of Soviet troops."

Jake accepted the pan, set it in place at the top of the stack, turned back and leaned nonchalantly upon the tailgate. The morning customers for coffee and husks were gone. Now the market was almost empty. A few stragglers stepped hesitantly over the rough ground, picking at the paltry items on offer.

Jake was stationed as he had been instructed, between two other trucks also bearing hardware and household goods. Their vehicle's front bumper rested close to the single remaining wall of an office building; above their heads were the ghosts of a few placards proclaiming the proprietor who had lost all in the war. Crumbling relics of walls extended to either side, forming a mini-tunnel into which he had nosed his truck. This position offered them a semblance of privacy and distance from their neighbors.

Jake kept his face immobile as Hechter swiftly sketched out their journey and the contact, his eyes flickering in bored fashion over the few would-be shoppers. If there were watchers, Jake could not identify them. Even their neighbors gave them little mind. They had paid their dues like all the others and been assigned a spot and merited little further concern.

Hechter reached the point where they had spoken from the ditch and said, "Your wife was most concerned that you had not accompanied us."

"I can imagine."

"More than concerned. She was distraught. It took the major quite a time to calm her enough to make plans."

"What major?"

A trace of humor came and went within the depths of Hechter's clear blue eyes. "He said that you would probably ask that very same question."

In a voice so low that it scarcely carried to Jake, much less to the people around them, Hechter related the little that he had gathered from the pair while remaining hidden in the ditch. How there had been a leak, probably a spy, within NATO intelligence. How their local operatives had not been simply sent elsewhere, but rather eliminated. How Jake himself might already be compromised. And how the Russian officer had ordered Sally and the major to leave by noon and not return.

"I have to tell you," Hechter finished. "Your wife was less than impressed with your reason for not coming."

"No," Jake agreed quietly. "She wouldn't have been."

"She told me to remind you of the promise you made to her before your departure. She said that several times."

"I remember," Jake murmured, his heart aching. "One thing I don't understand, though. Why couldn't they take you, too?"

Hechter shifted his gaze. "They could."

"So?"

"I decided," Hechter said slowly, "that I owed you a message."

Jake inspected the scientist, wondered at his own inability to overcome his aversion and offer the man a simple thanks. But in that single glance toward Hechter's proud features, Jake found himself again confronted by the specter of the past and what he had lost. The anger simply would not let him be.

A querulous voice startled him by demanding, "Well? Are you open for business, or is this gossip of yours going to continue on all day?"

Jake swung around, then lowered his eyes to meet the impatient gaze of a woman as broad as she was high. Two beefy arms rested propped upon her ample hips. A pair of legs thicker than his waist were planted in the rocky soil. Jake started to comment about her not appearing to have suffered overmuch from a lack of food, then changed his mind. The woman looked like she packed quite a wallop. "What can I do for you, mother?"

"Mother, is it now? You'll not be garnering a higher price from me with those fancy words of yours, gypsy. That I can promise you for sure." She stepped forward, shouldered Hechter to one side, and went on loud enough for the neighboring trucks to hear, "I've a need for a skillet. One large enough to cook for a hungry man and six children determined to eat everything the cursed war has not destroyed."

"Then you'll be after this one," Jake said, shifting the pile around and hefting a cast-iron pan fully two feet across. "The finest you'll find anywhere."

She accepted the long handle, grunted noncommittally, and demanded, "So how much do you want to steal from a defenseless old mother, then?"

"You're the one who'll be doing the stealing," Jake replied, taking in the steel-gray bun, the hands so chapped they had swollen to almost twice their normal size, the determined set to her chin. "You'll not find a lower price anywhere."

"If that's the case, then perhaps I could find means to buy more than one." Her back to the market, she leaned over, rattled the pile of pots, asked quietly, "Do you have the Bibles?"

Jake faltered for a second time that morning. "What?"

"The Bibles, man, the Bibles." Her voice carried the continual hiss of a scalding teapot. "Don't you dare tell me that blind bear of a man sent me to the wrong truck."

"No, no," Jake muttered, collecting himself. "I have them."

"Then listen. Set them in the space between the

front of your truck and the wall."

"But how—"

"Just do it, and if you want to save your own worthless hide, you'll take your lunch in the same spot." She wheeled about, said more loudly, "You're as big a thief as the rest of them."

"Take it or leave it," Jake said flatly, his voice as loud as hers.

"Aye, there it is," the huge woman said bitterly, handing him a tightly folded bundle of notes. "No choice at all for the likes of me, is there."

Jake made a pretense of counting the bills, shoved them in his pocket, hefted two of the larger pans, recognized genuine avarice in her gaze when he passed them over. There was need here, as well as subterfuge. "Wait," he said.

He scrambled into the truck and came out with three pairs of children's boots. He piled them on top of the pots in her arms, was pleased to see her eyes open larger and her voice say softly, "Shoes."

"A gift," he declared loudly. "All I ask is that you tell your friends, those with money, that here stands an honest trader."

"Huh!" she snorted. "And how many would a woman of my means know who have money? Saved all winter for these pots, I have." Then she pretended to shift the pots for a better grip, making a racket in the process, and saying swiftly, "All the shoes up with the Bibles. But none of the pans. Too much noise."

Jake nodded, pretended to help her organize her load, asked, "What's happening this afternoon?"

"Questions for later." She took a step back, stopped to eye him up and down. "It's not often I have to make a second judgment, especially of a gypsy and a man of the road. But I'll say to all who ask, it's a pity we don't have more like yourself."

"Good day to you, good woman," Jake called after her, conscious of the eyes. He then made a pretense of inspecting the almost empty market lot before turning to Hechter and proclaiming loudly, "Is that to be our only customer of the day? I've seen more activity in a morgue."

He motioned for Hechter to climb on board. "Get up there and start handing me down things. We might as well clean the truck as stand around here looking miserable."

Attention soon turned elsewhere, as Jake piled the pots and pans about his feet, then began accepting the bales of shoes and feed and taking them up front. With swift motions he shifted the secret handle, then started pulling out the burlap sacks of Bibles. There was nothing on the outside to differentiate these sacks from those holding the shoes.

By the time the compartment was empty and re-sealed, both men were puffing hard. Jake handed him a rag and said quietly, "Just move the dirt around as you wipe. Best to keep the doors hidden even if they are empty."

Hechter nodded and set to work, all his former bluster silenced. Jake watched him work and wondered again at his own lingering resentment. The man had clearly apologized as best as he was able. He had even returned to tell him of the contact with Sally, when all reason and self-interest would have urged him to escape. Yet here Jake stood, trapped within emotions which both reason and his own faith told him were not only wrong, but also unworthy. But telling himself these things did nothing to free him from what he felt, nor dim this flame of anger whenever he looked in Hechter's direction.

Jake waited until Hechter had settled down beside him, then asked quietly, "What was the real reason you came back?"

Hechter started to reply, then caught himself, looked beyond Jake, and his eyes grew wide. Before Jake could turn around, a tremulous woman's voice replied, "Because I begged him to."

Chapter Fifteen

D on't be mad with me. Please. I couldn't stand it just now."

"I'm not mad," Jake replied, and continued to hustle her up front. But when they approached the wall, Jake stopped cold, looked about, asked, "What is going on around here?"

"I couldn't go back without you. I just couldn't." Sally's features played halfway between stubborn defiance and a teary-eyed plea. "So I staged a fight with Theo, that's the major—well, only half staged, because he said I was being a total fool and might jeopardize your safety, but I didn't care, I don't care, I couldn't leave you here with goodness knows what's about to happen."

Jake walked around the space in front of the truck where he had left the sacks of shoes and Bibles. The space was completely empty. He inspected the wall, found it as rock solid and unyielding as before. "I don't understand any of this."

"I just walked off. The Russians didn't try to stop me. Their orders must have been about Theo and the truck, or maybe they were just worried because it was getting toward eleven-thirty and we had to be back by noon. The roads coming here were empty. Totally, completely empty. I wasn't stopped once. I came straight here. There aren't even any policemen down on the street in front of the market. Nobody." She reached over, stopped Jake's baffled gaze about the space in front of their truck, said, "Tell me you're not mad."

Hans stepped up beside them. "It's just gone noon." He looked around the area, demanded, "Where are the goods?"

"I was hoping you could tell me that," Jake replied.

"Jake, please, would you look at me and—" Sally stopped with a little squeak. She hopped back a step and sat on the hood of the truck. "The ground just moved."

A section of the dusty earth came up, pushed aside, and revealed the scraggly dark beard of the one-eyed man. He nodded at Jake, jerked at the sight of Sally, demanded quietly, "What is she doing here?"

"Long story."

"No time. Come, quickly, all of you. And watch your step. There are rats."

"Berlin has become a microcosm of all Europe," the burly man was saying. "This was Stalin's decision. What happens here will determine what will happen first in Germany, then France, then Italy. Then, my friend, it will be too late."

"Too late for what?" Jake still had difficulty fitting together the jumbled pieces confronting him. This one-eyed man and his precise speech. The surroundings, the atmosphere, the urgency with which this man spoke.

"Too late to do what must be done," he replied.

Before he could continue, Sally interrupted him with, "Where is everybody?"

He looked at her. Clearly he was unsure what to think of this woman and resented her presence. "We have sent everyone home until the emergency has stabilized. It is safer."

"What emergency?"

"All in good time." The man returned his attention to Jake. "You hold to the same error as most of your countrymen. I saw this coming, as did others. In order to fight the war with Stalin's Russia on your side, you chose to overlook the kind of man with whom you dealt. Now it is hard for you to accept the truth."

"And that is?"

"That this man is your enemy. And not just yours. He is the enemy of all freedom. And all faith."

A bear, Jake decided. That was what this Karl Schreiner most resembled. A big hairy bear, scarred from countless battles and carrying the burden of things which Jake could only imagine. He ventured a guess, "You were on the Russian front?"

"I was. And walked home when it was over, seven months on the road through ice and snow and mud and rain, with hunger and pain as my only companions." Karl started to scratch at his blind eye, caught himself and lowered his hand. "You think this is what has caused me to think the way I do? Listen, my friend. Stalin's world has no room for faith in anything but Stalin. He may dress his lie up in other words, like brotherhood or Communism or Mother Russia. But in truth Stalin is the new Caesar, setting himself up to be worshiped and made a god on earth."

Faith. This was the most jarring fragment of all. The

man claimed to be not just a believer, but a lay minister as well. They sat together in a stone-lined office. Beyond the stout open door was what had become a meeting hall and before had been the wine cellar of a gracious manor. The manor was gone, the wine racks now stacked with Jake's Bibles, as well as clothes and shoes and medicines and children's toys.

Sally interrupted them again. Her voice was soft and tired, yet somehow stronger because of the effort it took to speak. "Jake and I are believers."

Surprise registered on the broad-bearded features. Karl looked from one to the other. "This is truth?"

"It is," Jake confirmed. Proud of her. So glad to be with her that for the moment, for this tiny sliver of time and safety and comfort, there was no room for worry or condemnation. She was here. It was enough.

Narrow windows lined one wall of both the office and the meeting hall, permitting in meager afternoon light. The ceiling in the hall was high and vaulted, rising in great stone arches which intersected before descending to sturdy pillars. The benches were hard and wooden and still bore the marks of vineyards which had supplied the crates from which they were made. The room was unadorned save for a single large cross, the timbers taken from the derelict manor, rough and scarred by war and bombs. Jake found his gaze repeatedly drawn through the office doorway and out to that war-scarred cross, as though there were a message being whispered to his heart, something he either could not hear or was frightened to accept.

Karl gathered himself and went on, "The West sits at the table and argues about border disputes and the fact that they can no longer move easily through the eastern sector of Berlin. But this is just a smokescreen.

It is intended to keep you occupied while other, greater operations go unnoticed."

"What operations?"

"This is what I shall have to show you." He rose to his feet. "We leave in fifteen minutes."

Sally waited until Karl had moved off before asking, "What do you think?"

"I don't know." Jake looked at her. She had not released his hand since descending into the sewer and watching the burly man and his assistant slide the segment of false flooring back into place. "How are you feeling?"

"Tired," she said, and showed it. Her face bore the finely etched lines of extreme fatigue and tension. "I don't think I've really slept since this started."

"Do you want to rest?"

"Later." Her eyes rested calmly on Jake as she declared, "I trust him."

He nodded, accepted the information, said, "You've changed since we've gotten here."

"What do you mean?"

"You were a frightened little mouse back at the truck," he replied.

"I was afraid you were going to try and send me away," she said, her fingers linking themselves more tightly with his. "I didn't want to fight with you."

He freed one hand to trace a feather-touch down the side of the frame made by her tousled hair. "I'm glad you came."

The haunted look returned, flitting across her features like clouds across a windswept sky. "After you left England, I found myself lying there awake at night, facing changes. Some nights I felt like it was the only thing that kept me intact, feeling like I needed to use this time to make these realizations and build for the future. A future together. Otherwise I might have drowned in my fears that you wouldn't . . ."

He stilled her words with a finger to her lips, or tried to, but she shook her head. Whatever it was, it needed to be said. Jake settled back, filled to bursting with the wonder of being so loved.

"I've always been independent, determined to go my own way and be my own person. I never thought being married would change this. But it has. Before, I thought it was going to be just fine, you'd go off on your own little adventures, and it would give me the space to be myself. But it won't work, Jake. I'm too much a part of you." Sally leaned over far enough to place her head on his shoulder. "We have to do something about this, Jake. I'm not asking you to change. I'm only asking for you to make it so whatever it is you need to do, I can do it with you."

"I understand," he murmured. He did.

A sharp knock sounded on the door. Karl pushed through, every action fueled by his impatient strength. He looked at Sally, said, "You and your husband may take my quarters. They lie beyond the kitchen and the dorm where your Hans Hechter has bunked down. I suggest you go rest." His attention swiveled to Jake. "Time to move."

"Anyone who lives by faith in the coming days will have to be a fighter."

They were crouched in the same rabbit warren of sewer tunnels that had carried them from the market to the manor's bombed-out hulk. Overhead rumbled a seemingly endless train of vehicles so heavy they caused the walls around Jake to tremble. The only light came from a kerosene lantern in Karl's massive grip. The smell of burning oil helped to stave off the worst of the sewer's stench.

"That's what you were thinking, wasn't it?" the burly man pressed. "How one of Hitler's soldiers came to be sitting here beside you, a spy for the West and a soldier for God."

"There is a lot about this whole business," Jake replied, "which I do not begin to understand."

"God speaks to a man when he is ready and able to listen. For me, it happened on an icy field in the middle of nowhere, when death was as real to me as the cold that blistered my feet. He spoke to me then. I heard His voice, and I knew that I was to be saved." He thumped his barrel chest. "Not saved in the sense of living longer in this pitiful body. For an instant of clarity I realized that if I lived or died, it was *His* choice, and I was going to be content with the decision."

"I understand," Jake said quietly.

"He called me back here," the deep voice rumbled on. "Back to a city and a country as ruined by war as I was myself. Filled with needs which no human hand could answer. Desperate with hunger for the truth I had found and brought back with me." The single dark eye glimmered in the lantern light. "But it will take a fighter to be a Christian in these coming times. Make no mistake. Stalin's world has less room for true Christian faith than the Nazis did. Already the NKVD, the secret police, and their German minions called the People's Police have started their sorties. Invading houses of worship, stripping them bare. One Bible per church."

"What about the ones we brought?"

"We will not keep them long." He pointed toward the gradually diminishing noise overhead. "As soon as this moment of crisis has passed, we will distribute them to those who have lost everything. There are many such among us. It is the struggle that keeps me busy, seeing to their needs." Karl paused, squinted as he examined Jake, then went on, "At least, the external struggle. My internal struggle is far different."

"So is mine," Jake said quietly, the words coming out before he had realized he had spoken, as though the burly man's own confession was an invitation he had been waiting for. Jake found the growing silence overhead pushing at him. Urging him to open doors that he vastly preferred to keep shut. He found himself struggling to speak, and at the same time to keep still, unwilling to discuss personal matters with this man who had once been his enemy. And then he could not remain silent any longer. "I feel like I'm going back over the same problems again and again inside myself."

"I have sensed this struggle within you." The burly man did not seem the least bit surprised to hear such things, seated there in the dank putrid darkness of a Berlin sewer. "Yours is a common trait among believers."

"I thought I had left all this behind me," Jake went on. "But here it still is, worse than before."

"Not worse," the man corrected. "Seen in the fullness of its proper time." He set the lantern on the stone ledge beside him and rubbed two tired hands down the sides of his face. "Four months after I set up the *Evangelische Keller*, that is what we call our cellar church, I was approached by a group of neighbors. The rubble lot where once three blocks of apartments and an office building had stood was being taken over by black marketeers. There was liquor and fights and growing evil. Yet the people did not want the black marketeers to leave. They needed the goods. What they wanted was for me to control them. They knew I was a fighter, a former soldier, and most of those who remained were either women with children or too old or too infirm to do it themselves."

Karl's deep voice echoed gently up and down the concrete way. "I was terrified that I would revert to what I had been before. After all, I had only been a Christian for not even two years, and I had been a soldier three times that long. The only reason I ran the Keller at all was that none of the priests who had been carted off by the Nazis had returned from the concentration camps. None. Our little region of Berlin was without either church or minister. But my neighbors did not see me as a preacher. They saw me as a *man*. Someone who could be called on in their hour of need. My fears meant nothing to them. So what if I returned to my angry ways and fought and struggled and even perhaps killed again? They trusted me because I was a Christian, but they needed me because I was strong."

The stare was inward directed, the coarse features twisted with the power of his struggle. "I did the only thing that made sense. I prayed. I prayed and I waited, and as I waited I watched the situation worsen. Prostitutes began collecting around the market area, drawing in more of the war's refuse. So with my former comrade whom you have met, a man who has also now committed his life to the Lord, together we did what was needed. We cleared out the worst of the criminals and set out to control the others. We paid the bribes demanded by the Soviet soldiers and the German bureaucrats. We fought when we had to. We collected payments from all the traders, and with this money we financed the church. The only working church now in all this segment of Berlin."

"You did right," Jake said quietly.

"Yes? You are sure of this?" The fierce gaze turned outward again. "But what of the anger that is drawn out of me? What of this pleasure I feel for the battle and the struggle and the power in controlling this market?" When Jake did not answer, the gaze returned inward. "Then through church channels, through *church* channels, I was asked to send my assessment of the Communists' attitude toward the faithful. This led to other questions, about the rebuilding, the economy, the attitude of the people, the police, the effects of the Soviets. And then to helping directly with problems such as yours. I did not hesitate to respond. Yet I knew great reluctance. Not about the actions, about *myself*. All these activities were drawing out things within myself which I did not wish to see. I was confronted time and again with my own anger, with my own unsolved problems, with battles that still raged far below the surface."

Jake nodded slowly, his entire being rocking back and forth in time to the man's words. His words and experiences were different, but the struggle was the same. He felt that in his bones.

"How could this be? I was a Christian, I felt in the very marrow of my being that I was saved. Then how could I still harbor all these vestiges of who I had been before? Had I not accepted the call to repentance? Had I not dedicated my life to the Master? Did I not feel that sense of solid rightness to my deeds? Then why was I still so plagued by all of these storms in my mind and heart and soul?"

"You're not just talking about yourself," Jake confessed. "You're talking about me as well."

"Listen to me. I am talking about *every* believer. I do not have all the reasons, my friend. And those I have found may be valid only for me. But one thing I will tell you now, for I have seen the same storm in your eyes that has raged in mine. There is a purpose to it all. In the moment of greatest confusion, when the gale hurtles you about and all your questions are riddles without answers, remember the One who walks upon the waters. He calls to you to join Him, to do the impossible. He reminds you that in His gracious hands lies the power to calm all tempests and bring light to the deepest dark."

Karl picked up his lantern, lifted the glass face, and blew out the light. In the sudden darkness there was a grating overhead, followed by a sliver of light so brilliant that Jake had to shield his eyes. Karl waited for his own vision to clear, then poked his head up, inspected in both directions. "Come," he said. "It is time for you to see the new foe at work."

Chapter Sixteen

E verything is so quiet," Jake said. His voice was barely above a whisper, but still the sound rang loud in his ears.

"These people have long since learned when it is best to disappear," Karl muttered, his basso rumble kept low. "Even so, we must be grateful. It covers your presence in the chapel, which is a risk to all. We must find a way to send you on before people return to the streets and the sanctuary. Informers are everywhere."

They rode bicycles taken from a tumbledown storage shed set beside their exit from the underground passage. They rode down narrow ways, moving ever farther from the city. The condensed feel of a bombed suburb had been left behind. Their way was now lined by garden walls and stone cottages and occasional glimpses of open countryside. Their tires scraped loud over the gritty surface. They had seen no one since emerging from the sewer.

Jake was hard pressed to keep up with Karl. Despite his bulk, the man cycled along at a surprising pace. "What exactly is going on?"

"Exactly," the big man puffed. "Exactly, this afternoon Stalin sealed off Berlin."

Jake faltered, stopped, then had to race to catch up. "What?"

"They have created an island," the big man continued without slowing. "The western sector of Berlin is now surrounded by Soviet forces and is totally isolated. Cut off from all aid. Stalin has given the world an ultimatum. Relinquish Berlin, or face the consequences."

The late afternoon sky was blue and cloud flecked and preparing for a glorious sunset. Jake caught the faintest hint of noise. Familiar, yet strange. The noise drifted away as a puff of wind slipped between two cottages, then returned, louder now. "What is that?"

"The sound of doom, if you are not careful. What you in the West do not understand," Karl went on, the words punching out in time to his impatient strokes, "is that Stalin plays with men and power as others play with chess pieces. Berlin is nothing more than a pawn's gambit, a test of your resolve and strength."

The sound was now strong enough to raise the hair on the nape of Jake's neck. He felt the sweat trickling down his spine coalesce and chill.

"Berlin is meant to occupy the West's attention while Stalin prepares the bigger operation. It is intended to blind you, and it is succeeding." Karl halted at the base of a tall hill, slipped to his feet, and started pushing his bicycle by foot. "Hurry."

Jake jogged alongside him up a heavily overgrown trail which paralleled the hillside. There was no longer any need for quiet caution. The rumbling was as loud as thunder. "But what does he want?"

Impatiently Karl dumped his bicycle into a bush and started scrambling up the slope. Over his shoulder he tossed back the single word, "Everything."

The rise was steep, the ground loose. Jake grabbed handholds of grass and struggled to keep his footing. His breath came in punching gasps by the time he made the summit and collapsed beside Karl. Together they scrambled forward on hands and knees. Keeping his head low, Jake pushed through the final growth and saw a sight he had hoped was lost and gone forever.

This was not a convoy. This was an army. A continuous line of vehicles stretched out in both directions as far as Jake could see. The trucks were full. With troops. And munitions. And they pulled heavy guns. And tanks. Hundreds of them.

All headed west.

He had seen enough military convoys to know what he was witnessing. The troops were dirty and battle weary, but they sat upright and held their guns calmly, like seasoned troops headed into battle. The tanks and big guns were blackened with powder and dust, but all were clearly in working order. And all rolling inexorably toward the West.

But who was the enemy? And where was the war?

A second line of trucks was pouring eastward, but these held a different cargo entirely. They were filled to the brim with loot. Cattle trucks piled with so much furniture they could scarcely move. Paintings stacked like plywood. Bathtubs and sinks and toilets and kitchen stoves jammed together so haphazardly that most or all would be destroyed long before they arrived. Jake saw three trucks loaded to the gills with radios.

"The eastern sector of Berlin is being systematically emptied," Karl murmured, following Jake's gaze. "Telephones are loaded onto trucks with pitchforks. Away from prying Western eyes, Soviet soldiers wear watches from their wrists to their elbows and drape women's jewelry around their neck. Some say their superiors accept it because it keeps them from having to find money for back pay. What the Soviets cannot take or have no use for, they burn. Our skies are often black with the smoke of burning books and archives. The Russians intend to wipe out every last vestige of our past, both good and bad, and replace it with their own version."

A series of perhaps two dozen trucks paraded by below them, carrying what appeared to be an entire factory—machines, spare parts, even doors and windows. Behind them trundled a series of troop carriers, but these were filled with civilians. Karl went on, "Thousands of our most skilled workers are being swallowed by the Soviet whale. Whole factories are disappearing overnight. Last week we watched them dismantle and load up one of Berlin's telephone exchanges."

Jake returned his attention to the westbound flow as a series of massive eighty-eights rolled by. Some were being pulled by bulldozers, others by tanks, one by a series of farm tractors chained into tandem. There was no question about it. He was witnessing an army on the move.

He slipped back until his head was covered, turned to the bearded man beside him, and demanded, "Where are they headed?"

Karl fastened him with his good eye and replied, "That you and your Western allies must decide for yourselves."

•   •   •

Jake waited until they were back and preparing a meager supper before asking, "How do we get out?"

He and Karl Schreiner were standing to one side of the main hall, which saw duty as dining room, meeting point, distribution center, and place of worship. The place remained empty, however. Only Karl's stocky assistant and the heavyset woman, who also worked as chief cook, were present that evening. "I don't know. All my normal channels are now closed. We will have to wait and see what develops." The beard parted in a rare smile. "As you can imagine, we are learning to deal in impossibles. It is a part of working and living here in the east."

"That's exactly how I would describe this situation," Jake replied, looking around the stone-lined chamber. "Impossible."

"Hopeless," Karl agreed. "Incapable of being dealt with. By us, that is."

Jake examined this immense man with his vastly disfigured face, wishing he could understand such a strength of faith. "I could not do it," he said flatly. "Stay here and endure what you are open to."

Karl turned his good eye onto Jake and pinned him to the spot. "You could," he rumbled softly, "if this was what God had called you to do."

Jake's attention was caught by a block of wood nailed to the wall. The timber had been shattered by some awful force which had left one end splintered and the other charred black. A bomb, Jake guessed, destroying what probably had been the cross-tie to a roof of someone's home. Upon the timber the following words had not been carved, but rather branded, "Behold, I am the Lord, the God of all flesh. Is anything too difficult for me?"

"We are not a majority among believers," Karl was saying. "We are a select few. We have chosen to accept the call, to embrace the injustice of this worldly fate. To face the impossibility of living as evangelists in a world where evangelism is a crime. To be there and share the darkness with those who remain trapped by the world."

Jake glanced at the chamber's stone-lined windows. Carved in a continuous ring around one frame were the words: "For nothing will be impossible with God." Around the other frame was another inscription: "Jesus said, the things which are impossible with men are possible with God." Jake looked back to the hulking man, feeling the words' silent impact resound deep within him.

"God's power is unlimited," Karl went on, his voice too solid with confidence to brook doubt. "Let me tell you something about unlimited power. It means that whatever situation I face, I can do nothing better than to face it in utter emptiness."

Emptiness. Jake recalled his time in the Sahara, felt something of the same sense of strength he had felt in the desert. Yet there was something else. A whisper of distress disturbed the surface of his peace, like a wind blinding his vision with bitter desert sand. He confessed, "I have been thinking about the war. Not only that." He struggled to make sense of the disturbed vision in his mind and heart. "I'm still angry about it."

Karl's eyes searched out where Hans Hechter sat at the corner table, his hands cupped around a steaming mug, his shoulders sunk in what had come to be perpetual despair. The effects of Jake's blow had healed to a plum-colored swelling under one eye. "You did that?"

Jake nodded. Ashamed and yet defiant. Ready with a thousand arguments as to why it was right to have struck the man, yet filled with remorse. Not only for Hans Hechter. For something else.

Karl's gaze turned back to him. "You still carry the war in your heart."

Suddenly Jake had no wish to deny what he felt. "I thought I had left it behind, that I had prayed through it and found peace. But I guess I haven't."

The single eye probed with surgical precision. "Have you ever thought that this has come upon you for a purpose?"

Jake searched the massive bearded face. "No."

"Perhaps only you can reach that man over there. Perhaps your anger was returned to you as a means of carrying out God's call." He shrugged. "I do not profess to have all the answers. But I have often found that the Lord not only replaces the years the locusts have eaten, but also grants us opportunities to make gold from the lead of our lives. Do you understand what I am saying?"

"I'm not sure."

"Why not go and tell that man what is deepest in your heart," Karl suggested.

Jake took an involuntary step back. "Hans?"

"Is that his name? For a moment I forgot." The glittering eye gently mocked him. "For a moment I saw only another sinner who needed help to find his way."

Karl started to turn away, then stopped. "But of course, it would be impossible for you to give such help to a man like this. A *sinner* like this. An *enemy* like this. Of course. Think of all the horror this man and his kind have done to the world. Just think. How could anyone come to help one like this, much less confess their own deepest failings and weaknesses as a way to show that they too are human and in constant need of help?"

Jake wondered if the burly man could see how much his words had rocked him. "You don't ask much, do you?"

"Only the impossible," Karl replied softly. "Only the completely and utterly impossible."

Chapter Seventeen

Jake stirred in the night, eased his position on the lumpy straw mattress. Sally was instantly alert and looking at him. "What's the matter?"

"I can't sleep," he whispered.

"I know you can't sleep." She shifted to her side, raised her head up so that she could look down on his face. "Your not sleeping has kept me awake all night."

He heard her words as an invitation, a gift. "I feel like I'm being torn in two," he confessed.

"Why?"

Jake looked at his wife. Sally's eyes were luminous mirrors in the soft light, showing him his soul's recesses, secrets which had remained invisible throughout the days and the struggles. "Something inside of me keeps saying I need to talk to Hans Hechter. Not just talk. Share with him. Tell him about faith."

"Then you should." Quiet. Definite.

"It's not that simple."

"Yes it is."

Jake shook his head, tried to put concrete form to his tumultuous thoughts. "I keep thinking about my brother. How he died fighting everything this man stands for."

"Stood for," Sally corrected him quietly.

"I wonder," Jake said. "I really do. I mean, just look at the guy. Tell me you don't see a Nazi."

Sally kept her eyes fastened upon him, her gaze softly penetrating. "You know what I see? A man who holds to the past because he hasn't been offered anything to take its place. Yet."

The truth of her words raked across Jake's soul, exposing much that he would have preferred to keep hidden. Even from himself. He sighed, his eyes closed, trying to hold back the tide of awareness that came flooding in.

But Sally was not finished. "You know what else I see?"

"What?" he said, the word a sigh without beginning or end. An admission that he needed to hear what she said, no matter that it stripped him bare.

"I see a very great man given a very great gift." She paused long enough to gentle his protest with a kiss. "I see you being granted an opportunity to work through something really important. I don't know what it is that's holding you back from sharing your faith with him, but I know in my heart it's important. Not for him, Jake. Important for you. Something that is just begging to come out."

The power rose within him like a ball of flame, searing his very being as it lifted from the depths of his mind and heart, entering his mouth, ready to come out. Finally.

But she stopped him with a finger to his lips. "Not to me," she said, her words feather light. "I'm not the one who needs to hear this. Talk to Hans. Show him that you are human. That you have failings. But that something has come into your life that gives you the power and the wisdom to rise above them. And to heal."

Jake found Hechter in the same corner as before he had gone to bed. "Can't sleep?"

The man raised his eyes from the empty cup in his hands, his gaze a blue-clad void. "I have slept enough," he replied slowly. "I feel as though I have slept through my entire life, building dream upon dream."

Jake walked over and sat down across the rough-hewn table from the blond scientist, wondered what he should say, how he should begin.

"I feel," Hechter said, then dropped his head in defeat. "I don't know what I feel. My mind runs in circles, and it returns over and over to the war."

"I've been thinking about the war too," Jake confessed. "A lot."

"Colonel Jake Burnes," Hans said, the words taking a slow bitter cadence. "The hero. The victor."

Jake closed his eyes to the sudden rush of irritation, and in doing so had the wrenching sense of a turning. A small repentance. The words came to him as suddenly as the flood of peace, as though they had both been waiting, hovering just beyond reach, ready for him to make the turning. Away from anger, away from the past, away from all that was old and dead and dust. Repentance.

"I never felt so alive as I did during the war," Jake said quietly.

The power of his admission broke through

Hechter's self-absorption. His chin lifted with a jerk. "What?"

"War did that to me," Jake said, and felt a hot ballooning rush of emotion flood his chest. He knew then that he was confessing not only to Hechter, not only to himself, but to God. Giving voice to the unspeakable. "I became a Christian about five months after the war ended. Part of me looked for faith because of what I did in the war and what I needed to release myself from. Memories, pains, burdens that I did not want to carry for the rest of my life. Experiences that had branded me, warped my mind and my heart and my spirit. Left me feeling crippled inside."

"This I understand," Hans said, his voice so soft that the words were almost lost in the sputtering of the lantern overhead.

"But another part," Jake said, and had to stop. So much was filling his entire being that breath was hard to come by. He looked out over the shadowy hall to where the words had been inscribed around the second window. Everything is possible with God. The words flickered and danced in the lantern light, taking on a joyful life of their own. *Everything*.

"Part of me was missing something," Jake went on. "Not the war. But how the war made me feel. More than alive. *Vital*. In those moments of combat, there was something I never wanted to think about because I knew it was wrong. But not thinking about it did not make the feeling go away."

He stopped, his chest so tight he had to search the chamber for breath. There was nothing else within him except the need to see that part of himself for what it was, and understand. "It was," he hesitated long, his voice raw from the effort. "It was almost ecstasy. Horrible, worse than death sometimes. But totally overwhelming. Totally *now*."

The silence lasted long enough to become a part of the night, like the shadows and the flickering lantern and the rough-hewn table and the burning pain of his confession. Finally Hechter strained against the night's hold and asked quietly, "This faith of yours, has it offered you the same ecstasy?"

"Not the same at all. So different it has been possible to pretend that the other never happened. But it did. And I see how some warriors come to think of battle and God together in their minds."

"But you don't?"

"They are opposites," Jake said, and stopped to swallow. His throat felt sandblasted. Hans offered him a cup, Jake accepted and drank without looking, without realizing he was drinking. He set down the cup, went on, "The presence of God has given me at times what the word ecstasy is *supposed* to mean. In such moments, it is not something outside myself that forces the world to disappear. It is the Spirit of God himself, granting me one small instance of knowing what it means to be truly selfless. Without self. Open and exposed not by life-threatening horrors, but by *life*. Pure, complete, eternal life."

Slowly Jake raised himself to his feet, surrounded by the emptiness of unburdening. His soul felt ripped asunder. "In those moments," he said quietly, his voice directed to the dark window, "everything seems so simple, and God feels so close. Then something like this happens, and God is a billion miles away, and I am trapped inside all my mistakes and my sins and my failings. And all I can do is try and remember that even though I am the most unworthy man who ever lived, still He has forgiven me and brought me back into the eternal fold."

Jake felt as though there were a hundred other things a better man could have said. But for him the time was over, his own weaknesses too overwhelming to continue. "Good-night," he said, and began shuffling away.

He was almost to the hallway entrance when a quiet voice behind him said, "Colonel."

Reluctantly Jake turned back, and met Hans Hechter's gaze for the first time since beginning his confession. The scientist watched him calmly, the blue eyes empty of both pride and shadows. He sat beneath the flickering lantern, nodded his head slowly, and said, "Thank you."

Chapter Eighteen

It was a totally different Hans Hechter who woke him. A frantic, frightened Hans. Shaking him roughly, hissing softly, "Up, get up! We must flee!"

Sally was already out of bed and flinging clothes over her nightgown while Jake was still fighting off the fog of insufficient sleep. "What time—"

But hands were already jerking him up and onto his feet. "They have found me," an anxious voice whispered as Sally came around the bed and began tossing clothes at him.

"Who?" Jake's mind moved a half-step behind his fingers, which was why he buttoned his shirt up lopsided and tried to fit feet into the wrong shoes.

Hans was bundling him toward the door when it exploded inward and the heavyset woman hurried in. Her nightshirt was as great as a sail, and it billowed out around her as she shouldered past. "Down the back," she whispered. "Through the closet, into the sewers, hurry." Then she slid into bed, pulled the covers up to her curlers, and commenced to wave them frantically out and away.

With Hans pulling and Sally pushing, Jake had little choice but go with the flow. His mind remained sluggish, and his feet scuffled blindly until two steps into the hallway he heard the ice-chilling voice. "I asked you a simple question, Herr Schreiner. I suggest you not try my patience any further. Did you or did you not speak with a certain trader at what the locals call the chapel market?"

The cadaver. Jake came awake with electric suddenness, recognizing the voice of the rocket plant's political officer.

"And I told you as clearly as I know how," the big man rumbled back. His voice sounded bored and sleepy and irritated with being disturbed. "I talk with every trader who comes through. It is part of my job of keeping order. Tall and dark hair and a strong face could describe a dozen of them. More."

"Your job," the officer sneered. "All right, then. He was traveling with one or both of these two men. Look carefully, Herr Schreiner. Your very life depends upon it."

"Ah, why didn't you say you had photographs." The bear's voice receded into the distance as together they scurried down the hall, ducked into the dank chamber used as a hold-all for medicines, lifted Sally up and through the hole which opened into the sewer. "Yes, this blond one. He looks familiar. But I'm not exactly sure—"

"Search the place," snapped the officer, granting Jake the adrenaline surge he needed to grab the lantern hanging on the wall, then lift himself one-handed up and through the hole and follow Hans and Sally down the dark concrete tunnel.

They stumbled around two turnings before stopping and lighting the lantern. Their faces looked strained and hollowed from the fright. Hans looked at

Jake and asked, "What do we do now?"

"I don't know," Jake whispered, his voice still shaky from the shock. "From what Karl said, the border is sealed tight as a drum."

"I have to go back," Sally said.

Jake shook his head. "We can't risk it. Not for us, not for Karl. He said there were informers in his congregation."

"I *have* to," Sally countered. "In the rush I left my passport. I don't have any papers."

Jake opened his mouth to criticize, then slapped his own pockets, and confessed, "Neither do I. Or money."

Back around the corner there was the faint sound of voices. Instantly Jake lowered the lantern's flame to a dull glow. The voices called back and forth in what was clearly Russian. Then there was the sound of grunting, the snick of metal on stone, the splash of footfall in water.

They turned and fled.

By midday they were running on empty. Stumbling in hunger and exhaustion, jerking at every sound, feeble with the fear that there was no escape.

There were checkpoints everywhere. Soviet military vehicles filled the streets not choked with rubble. Civilians went about their business with furtive haste, scurrying from place to place with heads bowed and eyes sweeping everywhere, jumping into shadows or doorways or ruins at the sound of approaching vehicles. In that, at least, Jake and Hans and Sally looked like all the others.

Twice they had circled back toward the ruined

manor and Karl's cellar, but they had been stymied by soldiers posted at corners and searching all buildings extending out from the chapel market.

Hunger gnawed at Jake's middle. They did not have a cent between them. Passing food stalls, especially the ones grilling black-market meat, was agony. He could not look at Sally's drawn and haggard face without feeling a rising panic. They had to do something, and fast.

They crouched in the doorway of an apartment building, hooded by makeshift repairs holding up the crumbling facade. Jake looked from one spent face to the other and felt his determination harden. "We've got to make a run for it. They can't be watching every inch of the border area. There has to be some place we can cross."

"Twilight," Hans said, his voice chalky with weariness. "At night they search with lights and dogs."

Jake looked at him. "You know Berlin?"

"Some. We are approaching the university. I have lectured there from time to time. Beyond that is the central city."

"How far to the western border?"

Hans closed his eyes, the strain of concentrating tensing his features. "The closest point is about a half kilometer to our left. Another half-kilometer beyond that, perhaps less, lies the Brandenburg Gate."

Jake gripped Sally's hand, willing his strength into her. "Let's go."

They continued to skirt the main ways wherever possible, but were drawn unwillingly onto the thoroughfares when smaller streets became impassable. On one such instance, Jake caught sight of something that caused him to pause. Sally took it as another alarm, and started to draw into the closest doorway. "It's okay," he murmured. Then to Hans, "What do you make of it?"

"I'm not sure," the scientist said uncertainly. "But they appear to be headed toward the western sector."

Jake continued to stare down the connecting street, watching as what appeared to be a continual stream of civilians headed down the thoroughfare paralleling theirs. All of them were headed west.

"Russians," Sally whispered.

They slipped around the corner, and continued holding to smaller ways. Another two blocks, however, and a caved-in office building left them with no choice but to return to the thoroughfare. This time they almost ran headlong into a Russian jeep. But they slipped back unnoticed. The jeep's four passengers were all watching one street over, where the tide of civilians was growing ever larger.

Jake waited for the jeep to pass, searched in both directions, then said, "Across the street, hurry."

"Where are we going?"

"Might be safety in numbers," Jake said. "At least as far as they're headed."

They crossed the thoroughfare, hastened down a narrow way, clambered over a hill of broken bricks and concrete, and stopped in the corner's shadows.

The stream of civilians had reached flood proportions. Hundreds and hundreds of people, most of them young, walked purposefully by. There was no talk, no banners, no anger or raised fists or clubs or pickets. Almost all the young men wore coats and ties, the women dresses and matching jackets.

Sally murmured, "What on earth?"

Jake shook his head, studied the determined young

faces, saw how the political police and the Russian soldiers lining the way watched but made no move to
stop them. He had no reply.

Then Hans pointed and said, "I know that man.
Come on!"

Before Jake could think of an objection, Hans had
already pulled him away from the shadow's safety and
out and into the stream. They worked their way over
toward an older bearded gentleman dressed in tweeds
and hat and starched shirt and tie. It was only on closer
inspection that Jake could see the coat's multiple
patches, the frayed collar edge, the caverns that years
of perpetual hunger had hollowed beneath the neatly
cropped beard. Still, the eyes were bright and intelligent, the hands active as he punctuated his discussion
with the pair of students who walked alongside him.

Then he caught sight of who approached and
raised up to full height. "Hans! What in heaven's name
are you doing here?"

"I should ask you the same thing," Hans replied,
falling in alongside the older man.

"We are leaving," he replied simply, his eyes upon
Jake.

"May I introduce," Hans said, and covered the hesitation by turning and placing a proprietorial arm
upon Jake's shoulder. Then his blue eyes glinted with
a faint trace of humor, and he went on, "Dr. Jakob
Burnes and Frau Burnes. Perhaps you are familiar with
his work on philosophy and metaphysics? He is quite
famous in some quarters. It did not save him and his
wife, however, from being rousted by our new masters." Hans indicated the old man with a nod of his
head. "This is Dr. Ronald Hammer, head of Berlin
University's renowned physics department."

"Burnes, Burnes, no, I can't say..." The old man waved his hand. "No matter. You are most welcome, of course." He glanced at Hechter's rumpled and dirty form. "You are in trouble?"

"I am a wanted man," Hans confessed readily. "As is Dr. Burnes and his charming wife. Can you help us?"

"Perhaps, perhaps not. We are, as I said, leaving."

"Who?" Hans demanded, matching his step to the old man. "Leaving what?"

"All of us," Hammer replied simply. "The entire Berlin University. This very day. Students, professors, administration, even most of the janitors. Sixty thousand people, more or less. We see the hand of oppression tightening upon us once again, and we are departing."

"Will they let you out?"

The old man nodded ahead, toward the towering Brandenburg Gate. "That," he replied, "we shall see soon enough."

The gate was a mammoth affair, huge pillars rising to support a vast and ornately carved frieze. Upon the broad platform raced a divine chariot powered by mammoth winged beasts, the charioteer raising the crown of victory high toward the heavens. The closer they drew to the gate, the thicker the crowd became. Dr. Hammer was clearly well known and was permitted passage closer toward the front. Hans and Jake and Sally kept by his side and allowed themselves to be drawn further and further through the throng.

"The Free University of Berlin, it shall be called," Jake heard a voice ahead of him say. Despite the crowd's vast size, the people were so quiet that the words carried easily. "We shall found it in the western sector, if they will have us."

"That is the university chancellor," Hans said quietly. "A very brave man."

Dr. Hammer continued his gradual progress forward until Jake was able to make out a very erect old gentleman in university robes and a great mane of snow-white hair confronting a red-faced Russian officer. "You are gathered without permit," the officer rasped, his German carrying growling Russian overtones. "You are breaking the law."

"Then shoot us," the chancellor shouted back. "Show the entire world what your true colors are." He waved his arm beyond the three tanks and squads of Soviet soldiers to where the western correspondents stood massed. A pair of flatbed trucks had been backed up as close to the checkpoint as they could manage. At least a dozen cameramen stood crouched over their apparatuses, filming it all. "Either that," the chancellor cried, "or stand aside and let us go. For go or die we shall!"

With that he nodded once toward the massed assemblage, then turned and started for the checkpoint. As one, the crowd surged forward behind him. The Soviet officer raged a moment, raised his fist in threat, but as his soldiers raised their guns, the officer glanced over toward the cameramen. The officer dropped his hand, barked an order, and stepped back, defeated. The soldiers lowered their guns and moved out of the way.

In absolute silence, the gathering herded forward, carrying Jake and Sally and Hans along with them. Jake looked around as they passed under the great gate, passed the raised yellow barrier, passed the correspondents and the western soldiers. All in silence.

Not even the newspapermen dared break the power of that quiet moment.

Then they were past, and Jake's chest unlocked, and he could breathe again. Sally turned and swept into his arms. Hans deflated from his stiff posture, his shoulders slumping so far his chest went concave. They were through.

Jake motioned for Hans to follow them. Together they worked their way to the corner of the crowd, past the first line of soldiers, and into the guardhouse.

"I'm sorry, sir," the guard officer said, his voice still harboring awe from the scene. "You can't come in here."

"My name is Colonel Jake Burnes, NATO Intelligence." Suddenly Jake found himself so weak he had to lean on the wall for support. "I was told if I made it through to ask for an Uncle Charles."

The lieutenant's eyes popped wide open. "Yessir, I know about that one. Corporal, shut the door. Are these two people with you, Colonel?"

"They are indeed," Jake said, weakened even further with relief of being known and expected. And safe. Finally, finally safe. He felt Sally sway and held her close as he asked, "Could you find my wife a chair?"

"Your wife? I mean, yessir." The lieutenant snapped to action, lifted the chair from behind the corner desk. "Here, ma'am, you look all done in." Then to Jake, "The whole army's on the lookout for you, seems like, sir. Every guard detail here gets a call from some brass over at HQ, wanting to make sure we know what to do if you show up. I mean, when, sir."

"And what is that?" Jake asked, fatigue granting him patience.

"Call General Clay or Colonel Rayburn," the lieutenant snapped out, then realized what Jake meant. "Oh, right, sure. I'll do it now, sir."

"Excellent," Jake said. "And in the meantime, ask your corporal to find us something to eat."

"No problem, sir," the lieutenant said, motioning toward the door with his head. A soldier jumped to comply. As he dialed, the lieutenant glanced in Hans's direction and asked, "They'll want to know who it is accompanying you, sir."

Jake looked to where Hans stood propped in one corner, gray with exhaustion and hunger and confusion and released strain. And new fears. Jake waited until the scientist reluctantly met his gaze before speaking. "Tell them," Jake replied, "I travel with a friend."

Chapter Nineteen

I f Berlin is abandoned, half of Europe will be in the Communist fold by next week." General Clay was a pepper pot of a man with a voice like the bark of a bulldog. "Heard that from a journalist this morning, and for once I agree with the press one thousand percent."

They sat around the general's conference table, his Berlin-based staff assembled and augmented by several other generals brought in for the meeting. The confabulation was not on Jake's account; it had been taking place almost continually since the Soviets closed off the city.

The assembled brass were clearly unsure what to think of Jake Burnes, dressed as he was in his dark trader's outfit, not to mention dirt and a six-day scruff. Sally's presence only added to the confusion.

"Tell me, ah, Colonel," one of the generals said, a deskbound model with belly to match. "Just exactly what makes you so sure that the convoy you saw was not simply headed for some gathering point, from which the return journey to Moscow could be commenced?"

"To begin with," Jake said, his voice grating with

fatigue and growing impatience, "this was not just one convoy. More like a full army on the move. I personally saw several hundred troop carriers, half that number of tanks, the same of howitzers. And the line stretched out in both directions as far as I could see. Sir."

"Oh for heaven's sake, Phil," General Clay barked. "The Russkies have done everything but camp on your doorstep and stick a tank barrel down your kazoo." To Jake he went on, "You're the only one among us who's had a gander at the other side since this thing blew up in our faces, Colonel. I don't need to tell you that the situation is more than serious. The city is virtually without resources. Our western sectors will begin to starve in less than a week."

The thought of that was too much for the general to handle while seated. He popped to his feet and began pacing. "More than half my staff are pushing for us to assemble and force our way through. What do you think of that?"

Jake stared at the man. "By land?"

"That's the idea."

Jake recalled the massed force he had witnessed. "Sir, I guess there's a chance that the Soviets would back down. But it would go directly against whatever plan is behind their buildup. And if they don't give in—"

"Then we've got World War Three on our hands." The general stopped his pacing long enough to rake the table with his gaze. "A chance we cannot take, especially knowing about the massed armaments which you have described." He resumed his pacing, muttered to himself, "No, what we need is a show of force that is totally overwhelming, yet at the same time does not deliberately challenge them. Show them we mean business, but keep from having to fire the first shot."

A voice from across the table started, "Washington—"

General Clay cut him off with an impatient wave. "Forget them. They'll still be dithering when the city starts dining on shoe leather. No, what we need is a decision we can act on now, immediately, and then ask Washington's permission later." The sharp gaze returned to Jake. "Any ideas, Colonel?"

"Well," Jake said, struggling to bring his mind up to speed. "Air power was always their weak spot, and I haven't seen many planes at all the whole time I was over."

The entire room came to full alert. A voice across the table said, "I can confirm that, sir. They've been on our back constantly for spare parts. Seems they can hardly keep a dozen planes in the air."

General Clay wheeled about. "Phil, how many bombers can you get off the ground?"

"Oh," the deskbound general shrugged. "Close to a hundred, I'd say."

"I want twice that number in Wiesbaden tomorrow." He stabbed his finger at another figure farther down the table. "Food, fuel, raw materials. Lots of them, George. Make up a list, but before you do, start organizing the first shipments. I want five hundred tons to arrive here tomorrow. Seven hundred by the day after. A thousand tons a day by the end of the week."

"But that's—"

"I'll tell you what that is," the general barked, and slammed his hand down on the table. "That's an order!"

Chapter Twenty

J ake walked over to where Pierre Servais stood on the garden's broad top veranda, playing host and greeting late-arriving guests with the stiffness of an honor guard. He stood resplendent in his dress uniform and his momentary isolation. Jake asked him, "Are you nervous? Exhausted? In shock?"

Pierre scanned the crowd below him and replied somberly, "My friend, I am far too embarrassed for any of that."

"Why, what's the matter?"

Pierre's features folded down like a stubborn bull-dog. "You mean, besides the fact that more than half our guests could not even get into the church for the service, it was so full? Or the fact that my own wedding was taken from my hands, so that my mother could combine forces with my fiancée and turn what I thought would be a small chapel service for a few good friends into a new village fête? Or the fact that every woman within twenty kilometers has been cooking for a week? Or that there are people here today with whom my parents have not spoken since before I was born?"

"Yes," Jake said, struggling to keep a straight face. "Besides that."

"Then you are right, my friend," Pierre replied. "I have no reason to complain about anything."

Jake took a step back as another tidal wave of relatives and friends and villagers whooshed through the house's back doors and enveloped his friend. Pierre composed his mobile features into proper lines, bowed, endured multiple lipstick stains, held his peace as he was crushed to one over-ample bosom after another. He nodded and murmured as the matrons in their ballooning dresses and unsteady hats and clinking jewelry fluttered about him like a flock of giant pigeons.

From the relative safety of the veranda's far corner, Jake looked out over the vast back garden. Pierre's entire family, down to the ninth cousin twice removed, had been enlisted into taming the former jungle. Now the acreage of grass was respectably cropped for the first time since the beginning of the war, and great trestle tables were spread out beneath the ancient fruit trees. From where Jake stood, it looked as though the region's entire population, from the oldest living inhabitant to the youngest squalling newborn, had turned out for Pierre and Jasmyn's wedding.

The house was decorated with flowers and plates of hors d'oeuvres. But the real action was there in the back garden. The tables literally groaned under their burden of food. Tiered trays loaded with steamed mussels and shrimp. Onion tarts big as tractor tires. Boat-sized tureens of bouillabaisse and potato casseroles that matched them in size. Mountains of home-baked bread. Garlic sausages thick as Jake's thigh. And three lambs roasting on spits by the back wall. Not to mention two entire tables given over to desserts. And a bedroom stuffed with reserves, in case any of the guests began to feel peckish after the main dining was over and the dancing began.

Jake looked down to where Sally sat alongside Pierre's twin brother Patrique and across from Pierre's mother and father at the central table. Both of the old people looked bemused, tired, and glowing with unbelievable happiness. Two impossibles had come to life, two miracles blazed across the heavens, and everyone was here to share in their joy. One son, for whom the funeral service had long since been said, sat across from them, alive and smiling and growing stronger with each passing day. The other had returned from Africa with the woman both considered the daughter they had never had, the woman he had sworn was rejected from his life forever but today had taken as his wife.

Sally caught his eye, motioned toward the empty seat to her right. From her other side, Theo Travers gave a mighty grin as he toasted Jake with a brimming glass. Pierre's parents remained vague on exactly why Jake and Sally had arrived with this stranger in tow, but had latched on to the single word, hero, and used that as the introduction to all who were brought around.

Jake nodded toward them, raised one finger. Strange that he could find this moment of calm and isolation in the midst of such a celebration. He looked down at his wife with love and thanksgiving, knowing he was here today in large part because of her bravery. But he was not ready to give up his moment of quiet just yet.

The five days since their return to Berlin had swept

by in a flurry. As soon as the scientists had been safely stowed aboard one of the departing planes, Jake and Sally had hopped on another. Theo Travers had insisted on using his connections at Wiesbaden, their arrival point in the American sector, to round up travel passes and train tickets. Jake had shown his gratitude by inviting him to the wedding.

Jake had no intention of hurrying back to England. He had nothing waiting for him there except the job of packing. He had forwarded his own resignation by military courier. The last thing he wanted was to give somebody a chance to involve him in the inevitable enquiry over Sally's actions. There was too great a risk that whoever tried to criticize her would find themselves dining on their own teeth.

"Jake." Jasmyn passed through the great French doors and floated over. Her ballet-length white silk dress was unadorned, save for a white lace mantilla pinned with pearls to her dark hair and a matching string of pearls doubled about her neck. She glowed with the calm, self-possessed beauty of a princess. "What are my two favorite men doing up here away from the celebration?"

"Waiting for you," Jake replied.

She smiled and shook her head. "This is one day when neither you nor Pierre will be permitted to remain apart and aloof and alone."

Before he could object, she placed a hand on his arm and said, "There is a man inside who wishes to speak with you away from the guests."

"Who is it?"

"He did not say. But whoever it is, you must promise not to remain away for too long. The place of the best man is beside the groom." She dimpled. "Except, that is, when he is dancing with the bride."

Jake walked through the wide-open doors and had to stop to adjust to the sudden lack of sunlight. Then he tensed as a stumpy figure separated itself from an alcove and came limping toward him. "I suppose I should be quite angry with you for disappearing like that."

"Harry?"

"Having seen the bride, however," Harry Grisholm went on, "not to mention the food, I suppose you can be forgiven." He offered his hand. "How are you, Jake?"

"Surprised," Jake said numbly. "How did you find me?"

"What good is twenty years experience in the spy business if I can't track down a friend," Harry replied, grasping Jake's arm and leading him through an open doorway. "Let us see if we can find ourselves a relatively quiet corner. I have something I'd like to speak with you about."

They walked through the kitchen and entered the back alcove which Pierre's father used as his study. Before they were even seated, Jake warned, "If you're here to get us back before some review, forget it. I've already resigned my commission."

Harry tsk-tsked and replied, "That letter was unfortunately mislaid before anyone besides myself and Commander Randolf had an opportunity to read it."

"Then I'll send another," Jake responded stubbornly.

"You may wish to wait until after you've heard what I have to say." Harry gave Jake his patented smile, the one which did not need to descend from his eyes. "You have heard about the success of our operation in Berlin?"

Jake nodded. "I found a *Times* yesterday. Three days old, though."

"The Berlin Airlift, they're calling it," Harry went on. "Four thousand tons of supplies each and every day. The Americans are flying from Wiesbaden into Templehof airport. The Brits are using the Gatow airfield. Even the French are managing to bring in a few supplies to Tegel and opening up their unused landing slots to us. All in all, a most satisfactory show of power and determination, all without firing a shot. The results are already evident, I am happy to say. Stalin has begun quietly pulling his troops back from the border."

"Say, that's good news."

"Indeed it is. What makes it even better is that General Clay has seen fit to include your name in virtually every dispatch he has sent back to Washington." The eyes twinkled merrily. "Which makes it most difficult for anyone else to condemn your actions."

Jake felt the first ray of hope. "What about Sally?"

"Ah. Well, as it so happens, both of our scientists were fulsome in their praise of the two of you. Again, the powers that be have decided that given the chaotic state of our organization, Sally's fast action might very well have saved our collective necks."

"You caught the spy?"

"Indeed we did," Harry proclaimed, the glint taking on a steely tone. "He happened to be Quentin Helmsley's very own number two. This unfortunately has left Helmsley himself in a rather precarious position, and unable to criticize anyone's actions at the moment."

Jake found he did not mind that news in the least.

"The passport, the travel documents," he pressed. "Sally's absence without leave, what about all that?"

"I beg your pardon," came the merry reply. "What about all what?"

Jake studied the little man, observed, "You're not finished."

"With you? I should say not. I did not go to all this trouble, first to clear both your good names and then to track you down, just to enjoy a wedding feast." Harry's face grew somber. "Stalin's threat has not been ended, Jake. It has merely been deflected. Churchill gave a speech the other day. He told the world that an iron curtain had descended, blocking all of Eastern Europe from view."

An iron curtain. For some reason, the words brought a chill to Jake's mind.

"What is more, Stalin has begun pressing forward with aggression farther south. He wants an empire which runs from the Arctic Circle to the Indian Ocean, and it is only with diligence and fortitude that we shall be able to halt his onslaught. Are you with us?"

"I'll have to talk with Sally," Jake replied. He did not need to think it over. All such future steps would be taken together, or not at all.

"Of course you will. This involves you both." Harry leaned forward, his voice quieted. "I have been asked to take a field position, heading up a major new operation. I want you to come in as my number two. I will put you in as a senior diplomat, but your primary role will be to run operatives throughout the region and gather intelligence. This we will feed directly back to Washington, as well as to NATO headquarters. It may also interest you to know that Major Servais is going to be offered a similar position, so that if you accept, you two might be able to work together once more."

Jake felt the prickle of excitement race through him. "Where will we be based?"

"Did I not say? Forgive me." The merry twinkle returned. "My dear Colonel Burnes, I would very much like for you to be my man in Istanbul."